# The Dark World

THE REVIEWS ARE IN

### *In the Heart of the Garden Is a Tomb*
Midwest Book Award Silver Medal Winner

"It is unquestionably one of the most engaging collections of short stories that I have encountered in the last five years."—M. Grant Kellermeyer, author, editor and blogger

"The author wields his words like a finely-sharpened blade; every word – indeed every detail – adds another layer of mystery and suspense. In short, not a word is wasted."—Ellie Mitchell, Goodreads Review

"Pawlowski does an amazing job building his characters and ensuring that every MC is his/her own person. They have their own backstory, personality, and way of speaking that he brings to life on the page."—Nikki Mitchell, The Book Dragon Blog

"This book was amazing, I loved that it was all short stories. It reminded me of *Nightmares and Dreamscapes* by Stephen King with a little fantastical elements. All these stories could be books all by themselves. I'll be reading more from this author!" –Tracee, Goodreads Review

### *The Vermilion Book of the Macabre*

"Joe Pawlowski is an artist. With words as his medium, he paints his dark tales so realistically you will have nightmares. This book is a 'must read' if you enjoy the macabre." — Barbara Taylor, Amazon reviewer

"There are dark beings on the outer edges of this fictional world that often make themselves known in particularly gruesome ways. There are demons and witches and little people with peculiar powers and they all add to the appeal of this collection of stories."—Dave B., Amazon Reviewer

"If you love horror then I definitely recommend reading these stories. You won't be disappointed."—Heather Bane, Goodreads Reviewer

"Just have to say: I bought it this week and I love it. Scary and beautiful." — Emanuel Mayer, Facebook

"Ranging from stories of evil curses, unfortunate circumstances, and harrowing monsters Pawlowski unravels a narrative where the characters are the anchor point, the setting is undisputed, and the darkness of these stories settles uncomfortably in the mind of the reader." — Blogger and YouTube personality Gloria McNeely

"A creepy selection of imaginative short stories that are well written and interesting if you like supernatural and horror."— Shonna Mantle Walker, Amazon review

### *The Cannibal Gardener*

"A quick and gory read with a surprise ending I did not see coming," —Irene Cole, *Well Worth a Read* website

"An exciting tale of terror to the very end."—Shelly Neinast, Goodreads Reviewer

"Fans of James Rollins will love this author. I can't wait to get started on his other books!"—Ashley Dunn, Goodreads Reviewer

"The ending comes with a twist you don't see coming."—Sterling Kirkland, Goodreads Reviewer

# Pale Blades of Moonlight

## Joe Pawlowski

Glint Media

NEW HOPE, MINNESOTA

Also by Joe Pawlowski

*Echoes From a Shoreless Void*
*The Vermilion Book of the Macabre*
*The Cannibal Gardener*
*Why All the Skulls Are Grinning*
*In the Heart of the Garden Is a Tomb*
*The Watchful Dead*
*Dark House of Dreams*

**Joe Pawlowski/Glint Media**
**New Hope, Minnesota**
**www.joepawlowskiauthor.com**

Publisher's note: This is a work of fiction. Names, characters, places, and incidents are a product of the author's imagination. Locales and public names are sometimes used for atmospheric purposes.

Book layout © 2017 BookDesignTemplates.Com
Book cover by SelfPubBookCovers.Com

*Pale Blades of Moonlight*/**Joe Pawlowski**
1st edition
ISBN: 979-8-9857407-6-9

For Danita Mayer

"…As the moon from some dark gate of cloud
Throws o'er the sea a floating bridge of light,
Across whose trembling planks our fancies crowd
Into the realm of mystery and night,—

"So from the world of spirits there descends
A bridge of light, connecting it with this,
O'er whose unsteady floor, that sways and bends,
Wander our thoughts above the dark abyss."

—Henry Wadsworth Longfellow, "Haunted Houses"

# Contents

# THE RAG AND BONE SHOP

"He made daring incursions into the realm of the unreal without renouncing his residence in the partly surveyed and charted region of what we are pleased to call certitude."
—Ambrose Bierce, "Beyond the Wall"

B et I could find something to spend some cash on in here." Theo Hooper peered through the dusty window of the secondhand store on Grand Avenue in St. Paul.

His cousin Gabe scowled. "There's nothing but junk in here. Why waste your money?"

"I want to look around."

Gabe huffed in exasperation but followed him through a glass door with a poorly painted slate-blue wooden frame. The glass bore the legend, "The Rag and Bone Shop."

"Let's go to Wuollett Bakery and get some bear claws," Gabe suggested, eager to join in spending the largess Theo had received from relatives for graduating from Meadow Lake Elementary School.

"In a minute." Theo said.

Theo, at eleven, was a year younger than his cousin and was the trimmer, more serious-minded of the two. He had brown-black eyes and straggling blond hair that fell over his forehead. He kept the hundred fifty-seven dollars in graduation money in a gold-colored money clip in the front pocket of his textured, fleece shorts, where pickpockets couldn't get at it. Whenever he came from New Hope to the Twin Cities, he had an inordinate fear of pickpockets, though the crime was actually rare in the area.

Gabe, the St. Paul native, on the other hand, was fearless, and some would say, more impulsive. Thick-set with dull clamshell-gray eyes and shaggy mud-brown hair, Gabe had, until recently, a twin brother named Wally, who was walking home one night from a Metro Transit bus stop on Summit Avenue when he caught a bullet meant for someone else. He'd died instantly. The shooter turned out to be a nine-year-old kid who'd gotten hold of his father's Glock G17 and decided to take out his girlfriend because she dumped him. The girl, also nine, was unhurt. This happened about a year ago. Gabe seldom talked about his brother or the shooting, all but pretending the incident never happened, but Theo could see through to the scars left from the loss.

"Hey, look at this." Theo held up a pair of binoculars that might've been surplus from the Second World War.

"Cool," Gabe said with no enthusiasm.

The Rag and Bone Shop was long and narrow, and packed with tables and crooked racks of clothing on wire hangers. There were well-worn shoes, dingy purses, an old clock radio, unevenly stacked paperbacks with blistered spines, scratched and stained furniture, cheesy art prints, and a cracked statuette of the Buddha, among other items. There was barely enough room to walk around in.

A customer, a portly Black woman in a faded print dress asked the salesman if there was a shade that went with the dusty crystal lamp she was holding.

"Tell you what," the man said. "Pick any shade you see, and I'll throw it in free if you buy the lamp."

She tapped an index finger to her lips and looked around the store, then pointed to the other side of the room and said, "That woven orange one looks nice. The one on the brass floor lamp."

The sales guy looked like he should be living it up in retirement instead of working in a grubby old place like this. Bald on top with long white hair tied back in a ponytail, he had a thin, ancient face and a flat-bridged nose with a fleshy tip. He walked over to the floor lamp and removed the shade.

12

"Five bucks for the lamp with that shade?" the woman said.

"Yes," the old guy said, smacking his lips. "A good deal for you."

She smiled.

Theo put down the binoculars and began rummaging through a box of dog-eared comic books, looking for old *Batman*s or *Silver Surfer*s.

"Let's go," Gabe said. "There's nothing you want in here."

"How do you know what I want?"

"I'm just saying."

"Give me a minute." So far, the box yielded only *Archie*, *Scooby-Doo*, and *Richie Rich*, but he kept digging.

The woman left with her lamp and lampshade, and the old guy focused on the boys. "Can I help you find something?" he asked.

"Maybe a tetanus shot after poking around in this garbage," Gabe said.

"Gabe! Behave yourself. Sorry, mister. My cousin didn't mean anything."

The salesman pulled a tight, thin-lipped grin. "You like comic books?"

"Certain ones," Theo replied.

"I'll sell you that whole box for eight dollars. No, make that seven."

Theo didn't have the heart to tell the old guy that these comics in this condition weren't worth a dime to a collector. "Have any others?"

The salesman smacked his lips. "I may have some in the back of the store. Let me see."

The boys followed him through the dim maze of castoff garments, musty odds and ends, and miscellaneous devices that had once shined but had lost their shine long ago. On a table near the rear door sat several unopened cardboard boxes. The old guy popped them open one by one until he found what he was looking for. "What about these books? Are they the kind you like?"

Theo examined the contents of the box. Inside was a stack of *Silver Surfer*s mixed in with some clothing. Nine issues all together, in plastic sleeves, in pristine shape. "This is more like it," he said, removing the comics from their nest of woolen scarves and polyester trousers. He examined each book closely, and they all appeared in near-mint

13

condition, issues five through thirteen. Silver Surfer, the sentinel of Galactus. The loneliest man in the universe. "How much for these?"

The salesman jutted out his narrow chin and scratched it, but before he could answer, Gabe piped up with, "Hey, mister, what's that up there?" He pointed to a cobwebby back corner of the ceiling where heavy boards were nailed. The planks formed a rough square, maybe four feet by four feet, covering up what looked to be an attic entrance.

The old-timer glared briefly at Gabe before his eyes softened and he turned back toward Theo. "Nine comics, nine dollars. How does that sound to you?"

"Hmmm," Theo said, barely containing his glee. It was a steal, but he didn't want to look too eager.

"If it's just an attic entry," Gabe said, "why's it boarded up like that? It's almost as if you're trying to keep something from getting out."

Now both boys looked at him curiously.

He smacked his lips. "If you buy the comics, I'll tell you the story as it was told to me."

"Deal," Theo said, fishing out his money clip.

They trailed the salesman to the cash register, where he deposited Theo's nine dollars and stuffed the comics into a plastic Walgreens bag. While the old guy's back was turned, Gabe swiped a neon-blue Bic lighter from the counter and palmed it into a back pocket.

"Years ago, this shop used to be a bookstore that specialized in the occult," the old guy began. "It was run by a Jamaican woman named Cassandra Tai. She had a boyfriend who sometimes beat her. Don't remember his name, but he was a mean man who left her scarred with his abuse. Cassandra had a salesgirl named Mags. Some say she and Cassandra were lovers." He held up his hands and turned his head to the side. "I don't know, and I don't judge.

"Anyway, Cassandra used to tell people that when she was alone in the store, she sometimes heard noises from the attic. The sounds of people walking around and talking softly, she was pretty sure, in Russian. Just for a minute or so, then the sounds would disappear. One day Mags, the more adventurous of the two, suggested they take a look. "Could be someone up there. Who knows?"

The old-timer looked around his empty shop as if making sure no one else was listening.

"So, they got a ladder, and Mags climbed up to the attic entrance with a flashlight and peeked inside. She screamed at what she saw.

"On the attic floor, inches from the woman's nose, lay a human skeleton, the eye craters of the skull gaping back at her. Beside it lay a blood-stained dagger, black candles, and a cowbell. Her flashlight's beam searched out a sculpture against a back wall: a scowling, demonic figure with writhing tentacles arising from seaweeds. Elsewhere on the walls were a poster of death angels with black wings and stark-white faces, and more than a hundred mirrors of different sizes and shapes, many smeared with dried blood."

"Holy crap, mister," Theo said, slack-jawed. "Are you kidding us?"

"No. This is what I was told. And then ... when Mags went further into the attic, she noticed, on the attic deck beside the skeleton, a pool of dried blood. It was a terrifying display."

"Did they call the cops?" Gabe asked.

"Of course. They called the police at once, and investigators went over the whole scene, taking away the skeleton and other evidence. It obviously was the site of a Black Mass or some similar ritual. The police believed the skeleton was a human sacrifice, but they never figured out who it was or who did the killing. However, they determined the skeleton and the blood stains were over a hundred years old.

"So, someone just boarded it up?"

"Cassandra and Mags boarded it up, afraid that whatever evil had been released by the Black Mass a hundred years ago might still be up there and might harm them. They were very superstitious people." Here the old man leaned forward and said softly, almost in a whisper, "Every now and then, I think I hear noises coming from up there, too. But maybe it's just my imagination."

LATER THAT SUMMER, Theo again visited his cousin in St. Paul. By then, he'd spent all his graduation money, save a twenty he'd managed to squirrel away. This time Gabe had some cash, too, earned from babysitting a neighbor's little girl, and once again the two boys headed toward Grand Avenue for a light lunch and a little shopping.

15

For those unacquainted with the street, Grand Avenue is miles of charming stores, restaurants, coffee shops, and bars that began sprouting up in 1890 when St. Paul installed a streetcar line there. Back then, the technology was still fairly new, and at first, some feared using electricity to transport people. What if someone got shocked? Or if sparks from the rails started a fire? Eventually, the citizenry decided streetcars were harmless (as long as you didn't get run over by one) and a convenient way to get around. As a result of this new sensibility, Grand Avenue blossomed and continued to do so even when, in the 1950s, the city removed the last of the streetcar lines.

Today, Grand Avenue—featuring toy stores, galleries of local art, florists, bookstores, eateries, and other unique shops—is still going strong.

For Theo, the street was always a veritable wonderland, an old-world bazaar of captivating wares from offbeat merchants. He enjoyed strolling around, peering into windows, and selectively choosing how to spend his few precious dollars. Conversely, Gabe was more blasé since he lived just a block off the avenue and could visit it anytime.

"Hey, look," Theo said, pointing to a familiar, dusty window in the distance. "It's the shop where the old guy told us that story about the human sacrifice."

"Looks like the place is closed," Gabe said.

They walked up to The Rag and Bone Shop, and all the lights were off, giving the shop innards a haunted, skeletal quality. A closed sign hung in the display window.

"Did you guys know old Stan?" a voice behind them said.

When they turned around, an Asian man in a Twins shirt stood smoking a cigarette, regarding them.

"Sort of," Theo replied.

"Well, I hate to tell you, but the old man died a week ago. Heart attack. They say heart attack or cancer kills most people. If I had to choose, I'd go with a heart attack. Lot less pain."

Theo leaned in awkwardly and nodded, hands in his pockets. Gabe just stared at the guy.

"So, what happens to the store now?" Theo asked.

The man took in a lungful of smoke and blew it into the air. "Probate, I guess. Stan never mentioned any family, so I'm not sure. The place will probably stay vacant for a while, and then they'll turn it into a yogurt store or some such thing. I doubt anyone would be interested in resurrecting the old Rag and Bone Shop."

A swell of melancholy riffled Theo

"Anyway, out with the old and in with the new, as they say. You boys have a nice day." Then he walked off, puffing on his cancer stick like some man of the world from an old black-and-white movie.

They strolled in silence. After a while, Theo said, "What do you think they'll do with all that stuff?"

"I don't know. Haul it to the junkyard, probably." Gabe suddenly stopped walking. "Hey, Theo."

"Yeah?"

"I got an idea. What if we snuck into the shop tonight and see for ourselves what's up in the attic?"

"You serious?"

"Sure, why not. What's the matter? You afraid of ghosts?"

Theo pulled a tight face. "Of course not," he lied. "But in case you hadn't heard, it's still illegal to break into someone's property."

"That's why we do it at night. Sneak in through the back door like a couple of ninjas. We're not going to steal anything. Just take a look upstairs. It'll be an adventure."

Theo swallowed. "It's just that…"

"Come on. Don't be such a wuss."

Theo felt his chance of backing out of this adventure slipping away. "How would we even get in? The place is all locked up."

"Leave that to me," Gabe said, grinning. "Me and my old pal Jimmy."

THAT NIGHT, WALKING THROUGH BACK ALLEYS and side streets, the boys made their way to the back side of the secondhand store. It was after midnight, and they stuck as much as possible to the night shadows. When approaching the door, Gabe pulled a chunky pry bar from beneath his sleeveless denim jacket. "My friend Jimmy," he whispered, holding up the bar.

17

"What if there's an alarm?" Theo asked.

"Then we run like hell." Gabe chuckled. He wedged the heaver's iron prong between the door and the jamb and wrenched sharply. With a crunch, the door popped open. "C'mon," Gabe said, slipping inside.

Theo looked around cautiously before joining his cousin.

Inside, The Rag and Bone Shop was all angular silhouettes and pinched gloominess. Outside, through the far front window, they watched a white van drive by. Aside from an occasional passing vehicle the night street was vacant and quiet.

Gabe placed his crowbar on a cluttered tabletop and clicked on a penlight. The beam scoured the ceiling before coming to rest on the cobwebby corner where the attic boards clung.

"How do we get up there?" Theo asked, feeling a little lightheaded.

The light roamed the store jammed-full with bric-a-brac. "Do you see a ladder anywhere?"

"No. Maybe if we just stack up stuff to climb on."

"Okay."

They cleared the surface of the table beneath the attic entrance. Then they placed a smaller table atop that one. They centered a straight-backed wooden chair on the smaller table. Theo tested the chair's seat by applying pressure with his hands and shaking it. "Looks pretty solid."

"Here. You hold the flashlight and hand up Jimmy to me." Gabe crawled onto the small table, then edged onto the chair. Grabbing the pry bar from Theo, he stood on the wooden seat and fit the pronged tip under the first board. He yanked, and one end of the board groaned free. "Watch out below," he said, prying off the other end. The board clanked to the floor.

A few more minutes and the remaining boards were gone, and the unshielded attic cover shined naked in the flashlight's glow.

"Okay." Gabe handed Jimmy back down. "Now, give me the light."

Holding the penlight in his teeth, Gabe pushed, and the attic cover lifted. He set it off to one side, then seized the opening's frame and pulled himself up. He disappeared into the hole's blackness.

Theo climbed up and nervously followed him. The attic was pretty much as the late Stan had described it. Barely tall enough for the boys

18

to stand in, it spread the length and width of The Rag and Bone Shop, tenting down the middle. Most of the wall space was taken up by mirrors, maybe a hundred mirrors of different sizes and designs, some smeared with dried blood. They glared back at the boys when the penlight caught their surfaces. Cobwebs and dust were ubiquitous.

Soaked into the floor near the attic entrance, ancient dried blood formed a dark kidney-shaped area about three feet by six. A half dozen upturned black candles and a brass bell sat close by.

"This place is creee-py," Gabe said.

Beside a nearby wall, an impressive if unsettling statue of some mythic goddess that looked to be half octopus rose from a stone bed of seaweed. It leaned threateningly toward Theo and Gabe. Whoever'd fashioned the statue had captured rage in the goddess' eyes and mouth.

"Think anyone's been up here since they took away the skeleton?" Gabe asked.

"I doubt it."

Just past the bloodstain, a broadsheet poster displayed black-winged angels of death gathered in a circle around the same octo-goddess represented in the statue. The yellowed and faded poster hung from a board on a near rafter. One corner of the poster had come loose and partially exposed what appeared to be writing.

"I wonder what's under that poster?" Gabe stepped reverently around the bloodstain to the poster while Theo followed.

Gabe freed the remaining corners of the broadsheet, and it rolled on its own to a loose tube as it fell to the floor. Beneath it lay a square of wood scrawled at the border with bizarre images: a three-bladed ax in a circle of fire, disembodied wings impaled with tridents and arrows, thorny vines entwining a horned crow, and at each corner, a three-bladed ax in a circle of fire.

"What do you think those are?" Gabe asked, pointing to the symbols.

"Sigils," Theo said. "They're magical emblems. I read about them in one of the Harry Potter books."

"Magical, huh?" He leaned in to study them, his heavy breathing filling a vacuum of silence.

19

Bordered by the sigils, carved words called out to a pagan deity or perhaps a demon. They read over the words without speaking them aloud.

"Queen of the trident, queen of the sea, monarch of murky depths, we yer loathsome, we yer vile, seek yer aid. Smile upon one of yer children and help him cross safely back from the place of the gone. Quaff the blood we shed for ye, dark mistress. It is the blood of our atonement, wretched dregs that we are. It is a drop of crimson in an ocean of chaos. Let it be enough to win yer favor. Drink of this offering and think of us kindly. Be propitious and allow us to bask ever briefly in yer holy radiance, mighty Dagon."

"This must be some kind of prayer," Gabe said at last.

The boys glanced at each other, blinking, then looked around the mirror-line attic. Gabe bit his lower lip, taking it all in.

"Let's get out of here," Theo said. "We've seen all there is to see." He started back to the attic entrance, but Gabe stopped him.

"Wait a minute. Don't you think we should light the candles and ring the bell and say the words, and see if anything happens?"

"Happens?" Theo replied, fighting to keep the tremor from his voice.

"Yeah, you know. See if it gets this Dagon to appear."

Theo could tell from Gabe's eyes that he was serious. "I don't know, man. It sounds dangerous to me."

Gabe laughed. "Oh, come on. You're not buying any of this black-magic stuff, are you? It'll be fun."

Theo tried to remember something about black magic he might have learned in his catechism classes at St. Alphonzo's, but nothing came to mind. "What if the cops show up and catch us here?"

Gabe laughed again. "No one's going to catch us up here. What's the matter? Are you chicken?" He bawk-bawk-bawked, imitating a fowl.

"Of course not." Theo's eyebrows scrunched, and he frowned. There was no face-saving way to get out of this. "Okay. Then, let's get this over with."

Gabe arranged the candles into a ragged semicircle along the far side of the bloodstain, then lit them with a familiar-looking, neon-blue Bic

20

lighter. The flames shined bright enough to light the board with the sigils and the prayer. Gabe pocketed the penlight.

"Let's chant it three times, and you ring the bell after each time." He handed the tarnished brass bell to Theo.

They knelt on the dusty floor and commenced the incantations. "Queen of the trident, queen of the sea, monarch of murky depths, we yer loathsome, we yer vile, seek yer aid…" and so on. Three times they spoke the words; three times the bell rang.

Then they waited in the gloom with bated breaths. Nothing happened.

"You satisfied, Gabe?"

"Wait a minute. We forgot something." He pulled a folding knife from his denim jacket, opened a blade, and poked his middle finger, drawing a globule of blood. "For Dagon to drink," he explained, squeezing out three drops, adding them to the ancient death stain. He snapped the blade closed and returned it to his pocket. "Let's see if it works now," he said, smiling maniacally.

Somehow, adding the blood made the ceremony more real to Theo, and he did not want to repeat it, but he was already kneeling and holding the bell, and the sounds of Gabe's chicken squawks were still fresh in his memory. "Alright."

Once again, they recited the incantation three times, accompanied by the peals of the bell.

Suddenly, it felt like the air was being sucked out of the attic. Static electricity lifted the boys' hair, and Theo's flesh bristled with a crawling sensation. Thundering cracks of lightning lit the room in brilliant white flashes that ricocheted from the hundred mirrors.

The bell tumbled from Theo's fingers, clinking as it rolled across the floor. He looked at his cousin who knelt beside him, and was met by a quavering mask of terror. Gabe's curled lips struggled to form words but only managed a horrible pantomime.

The knees of Theo's jeans grew damp. The formerly dried blood stain now oozed with fresh red that spread beneath him. He sprang to his feet, grabbing Gabe by the shoulder and yanking him up.

The flashing ceased, and the only illumination was again the gloomy candlelight reflecting from the spreading pool of blood. Theo's ears filled with a roar like trees being ripped from the earth. He turned toward the sound's source and nearly fainted at what confronted his sight.

The demonic figure was no longer a statue but a horrific, living creature. Its tentacles squirmed in the air. Its taloned hands clawed at them. Now Theo saw that the scowl the sculptor had fashioned for it paled compared to its true expression. Sheer hatred radiated from the creature's amphibious eyes, flared nostrils, and bared teeth. Theo could not imagine a more terrifying vision.

But then, still speechless, Gabe pointed excitedly to the pool of blood at their feet, and to Theo's further horror, a red-coated dome was rising from it. Slowly, a head came up, enameled in crimson that dripped thickly from its chin. The lips cleaved open in a sickly smile, and eyes of gray fixed on Gabe.

Theo couldn't control his trembling. The figure, now risen to its chest, reached out a hand from the tarn of red and extended dripping fingers toward Gabe.

"Gabe!" Theo shouted. "It's you! It's you!"

He turned and watched as his cousin again fell to his knees, wearing a visage of utter disbelief. "Wally?" Gabe said.

A headlong coldness rushed through Theo. Wally? Gabe's dead twin brother?

Wally stretched toward Gabe. "Take my hand, brother," the apparition coaxed. "I want to feel the touch of the living."

A new anxiety gripped Theo. "Don't do it!"

But Gabe ignored him, instead clasping his dead brother's blood-sodden hand.

Again, the attic went white with repeated dazzling thunderbolts.

Wally snatched his kneeling brother toward him, and Gabe gave Theo a panicked, sidelong glance before—with a viscous slosh—tumbling headfirst into the otherworldly pool of redness. Before Theo had time to react, both figures disappeared. The surface of the blood tarn roiled with their struggling.

Theo knelt and, throwing caution aside, plunged his arm into the thick, churning liquid. The feeling was unreal, as if in the bloody sludge, he'd touched a live wire. But his fingers grasped something. A shoulder? An arm? He pulled for dear life. The blood pit gurgled as he forced in his other arm, grabbed wildly for something to hang onto, and finding it, leaned back and yanked for all he was worth.

There came a sound like a gigantic boot being pulled from muck, before the tension lessened and the torso came free. Theo crashed to the ground, then rolled from beneath the weight and gore of his blood-soaked cousin.

"Gabe!" he said, shaking him by the shoulder.

Groaning, he stared through Theo as if in a daze, his denim jacket lost to the Netherworld.

Rising unsteadily, Theo looked around the attic, and it was as if none of it had ever happened. The candles were still lit, but the bell rested upright beside them, and the statue of the demon goddess had returned to stone. The blood spot was once again just a dry kidney-shaped stain, and all was calm and quiet in the dusty old attic.

"Let's get the hell out of here," Theo said.

THEY SKULKED BACK SILENTLY in the moonlight through alleys and between houses.

When they came to Gabe's backyard, they hosed off as best they could, washing most of the blood into the moon-silvered late-July grass. They snuck back into the house, stripped off their clothes and hid them. Then they changed into their pajamas.

As the boys slunk into bed, Theo worried about his cousin. Ever since he'd yanked him from that awful blood pit, Gabe hadn't said a word, just followed Theo's lead numbly, in zombie fashion. Theo worried that Gabe was in shock, and he wasn't sure how serious that condition might be. He could only hope a good night's sleep would return his cousin to the same old Gabe.

Then another thought seized him. What if the body he'd yanked from the pool of blood wasn't Gabe at all. What if it was…

He drew the covers to his chin and stared wide-eyed into the dark.

# IRIS

"'There is no exquisite beauty,' says Bacon, Lord Verulam, speaking truly of all the forms and genera of beauty, 'without some strangeness in the proportion.'"
—Edgar Allan Poe, "Ligeia"

He thinks I'm his friend, but I'm not. I merely abide him for the sake of convenience. Bobby doesn't demand that I serve him, sexually or otherwise. He has neither crude habits nor poor hygiene. And though he killed a stranger for pocket change, I can see he holds no ill will toward me or anyone else.

He just needs someone to listen.

"It was an accident," he says, repeating those words time and again like a mantra. Sometimes, he'll add something like, "The gun went off, and he was on the floor, staring back at me, lifeless," or "I was just trying to frighten the salesgirl. When I fired the pistol, I wasn't even looking where I was aiming."

These cages are full of men whose lives are forever altered by a split-second of bad judgment. Though I have to say, I'm not one of them. I committed my crime with my eyes open and conviction in my heart. And I'd do it again. For Iris.

Often, Bobby's narrative veers off into the land of make-believe, his mind no doubt damaged by the rashness of having fired that pistol. Here, he'll talk of an escape, of a cabin in the woods where he found a young woman enslaved, her children hideously deformed, her captor returning and catching him. He even gave this phantom a name: Salazaar. A huge red demon with purple splotches on its jawline and chest, and miniature animated heads on each shoulder. The entity so frightened Bobby with its raging that Bobby raced out of the cabin. There, police officers were waiting, and he gladly gave himself up, the sanctity of prison preferable to the clutches of the evil demon. Anyway, that's his story.

I pretend to believe him. Why not? In these cages, having an ally is always beneficial, especially one as young, tough, and strong as Bobby. Even if he's a touch insane.

Whenever he isn't talking, a peaceful silence descends upon our cell, and from my roost on the top bunk, I stare at the ceiling, hands laced behind my head, and swim in my memories of Iris; in her scent (she smelled like the flower after which she was named, though perhaps one overripe), and the cadence of her voice (melodic if somewhat slurred), and the richness of her soulful eyes (earthy brown, with one delightfully misaligned).

On my perch, I play back every moment, from the first time I saw her to the last.

Back then, I was a real-estate agent, selling homes in the Twin Cities area and contentedly collecting my commissions. That day, a mild June afternoon, I was to show a three-bedroom split-level on Gettysburg Avenue in New Hope, overlooking nearby Liberty Park. The house was freshly painted and roomy. The prospective buyers were from Detroit, a Mr. Harold Hardrock and his invalid niece, Iris.

The previous owners had replaced the front stoop with a cement ramp, which was fortunate given the niece who, I'd been told, had difficulty getting around. I remember standing by the front door when the cream-colored Honda Odyssey minivan pulled into the driveway.

The driver consulted his phone, looked up, and frowned at the number on the house before turning off the engine and climbing out. He had a pale, thin face and large eyes, was well into his fifties, and wore the countenance of a man imprisoned in a bleak marriage. He walked around to the far side of the minivan and helped his passenger alight.

"Mr. Hardrock," I said. "It's a pleasure to meet you. And your charming niece." It never hurt a sale to lay the pleasantness on thick.

The niece hid behind a black veil attached to a brimless hat, and her slightly oversized dress looked like it came from a Goodwill rack.

I pasted on a smile. "Did you have any trouble finding the place?"

25

He mumbled something dismissive and led the niece rather roughly by a forearm. She stumbled in her orthopedic shoes as she and her guardian approached.

From the start, I felt drawn to her. To her hooked, lobster-claw fingers, the indelicate stalks of her wrists, the stiff bow of her arms. The whole of her form veered crookedly to one side. Her dress, I realized, hung loosely because nothing short of the miraculous in tailoring could adequately fit the swells and bends of her figure.

Why I was attracted to this misshapen woman, I have no idea. I'd never before been enticed by the feminine grotesque. But Iris jolted me to the core, and I had to look away from her to avoid embarrassing myself in front of her and her uncle.

"What brings you to New Hope, Mr. Hardrock?"

"3M moved me to their Cottage Grove plant from Detroit," he said. "I'm not too happy about it, but it was either move or lose my job. New Hope is closer to the Twin Cities, and it's just a half-hour's drive to Cottage Grove."

More like forty minutes, even in ideal driving conditions, but I bit my tongue on this factoid, not wanting to discourage him.

I did wonder if Hardrock's transfer had anything to do with a shakeup resulting from the problems at 3M that was in the news lately. There was the multi-billion-dollar lawsuit involving cancer-linked "forever chemicals" that had allegedly leached into municipal water supplies. Then there were the nearly 260,000 lawsuits claiming the company's military earplugs caused hearing loss. And wasn't there something about a 3M executive facing an alleged window-peeping charge in Hudson, Wisconsin? The firm certainly had its share of black eyes recently.

Still unnerved by my bizarre attraction to Iris, I focused on the house.

Luckily, the real-estate agent monologue came easily to me, having conducted countless tours of countless houses over the years. I pointed out the beamed vaults, the abundance of east- and west-facing windows, the wood-burning fireplace, the freshly carpeted bedrooms, the spacious dining area, the sliding doors that opened onto the cedar deck, the backyard shade trees, the attached garage, and so on. As we proceeded on our expedition, I couldn't help noticing from the corner of my eye how Mr. Hardrock conducted Iris with an open measure of meanness. He yanked, shouldered, and jostled her, at times pitilessly.

When at last the tour ended, I led Mr. Hardrock back to the front ramp and glanced his way. I could tell he liked the place.

"Let me talk to my banker," he said, "but this appears to be in my price range."

We shook hands, and I gave him a business card. "Call me if it looks like we have a deal."

He frowned and nodded, then, with a rough tug, moved Iris back toward the minivan.

I watched her walk: her jerky strides, her mottled and lumpy calves, and the way her dress gently draped one jutting hip. I suddenly was a believer in love at first sight.

What had come over me?


MAVIS—THAT WAS MY WIFE—made me breakfast every morning. Usually oatmeal, toast, and coffee, with an occasional bagel thrown in to keep things from going too routine. I don't like eggs; I don't even like the idea of them. Mavis didn't like eggs either, and we bonded, as was often the case, on our mutual dislike.

Before meeting Iris, I would've argued that Mavis was the perfect mate for me. Besides sharing pet peeves (eggs, noisy eaters, people who text in movie theaters, line-cutters, etc.), we both enjoyed having a spotless home, well-mannered pets, and a healthy portion of Baileys Irish Cream (neat of course), while viewing television game shows during evenings at home. And, I would add, Mavis was still comely enough in her forties to—if not stop a clock—at least turn a few heads. Slender, symmetrical, shapely, with a self-reliance that shined in the way she moved, she'd always struck me as the ideal woman. Only now, sitting across the breakfast table from her, chewing my oatmeal, I wasn't so sure. Lately, she struck me as a regular Plain Jane.

"So, when do you close on that Gettysburg property?" she asked that morning, a week after my initial showing.

"Eleven sharp. Of course, I'll buy them lunch afterward to show my appreciation."

27

"This is the uncle and his niece, then?"

"Yes. Thought I might get other offers on the place, stir up a little bidding war, but that never materialized. It's just these folks from Detroit. Hardrock, the 3M guy I told you about, and his niece." I couldn't bring myself to say her name, not with my wife sitting just across the table.

"Still, you'll be pleased to collect the commission on the sale, no doubt." She smiled at me, and, for some reason, I found her grin annoying.

"Yes. They paid full price, so my cut should be around eighteen thousand."

"Not bad for a day's work." Smiling more broadly, she slid a spoonful of oatmeal between her teeth.

ALL MORNING AT THE OFFICE IN EAGAN, I WAS NERVOUS. I told myself I'd be alright, that I'd get through the closing with Iris present without making a fool of myself. But as the hour approached, I became increasingly agitated.

My first tip-off that others could view my discomfort came when Janna Higgins, my administrative assistant, asked me if I felt ill. "You look feverish," she said, removing her aviator spectacles in an expression of concern.

I felt feverish, I had to admit. "Touch of a cold maybe," I said, "or allergies. Did you get that paperwork ready for the Hardrocks? They'll be here any minute."

She hurried off, and I went to the bathroom to splash cold water on my face. When I came out, Harold Hardrock and Iris were waiting in the reception area. He was dressed in business casual attire, and she had on the same dress she'd worn to last week's showing, including the dark veil that covered her features and lent her a certain mystique.

I shook his hand and nodded to her. "It's a pleasant day, don't you think?" I said as I escorted them to the conference room.

"A bit overcast and coolish, if you ask me," Hardrock said, all but dragging Iris through the door behind him. The way he manhandled her raised a flash of anger in me, but I did my best to hide it. He held the

28

purse strings, and he could still back out of the deal on a whim. I'd seen it happen before with prospective buyers.

We took seats at the conference table. Janna brought in the paperwork and took orders for refreshments.

"Water would be nice, thank you," Iris said. This was the first time I'd heard her speak, and to me, it was as if someone had strummed a harp in the room, so enchanting was her mumbled voice.

Hardrock asked some standard questions, and I gave him standard answers. I told him where to sign and where to initial, and he did. Then Iris, with a delicate clawed hand, took the pen from him and herself signed slowly and deliberately.

Once the formalities were over, I offered to take them to lunch. "Anywhere you like," I said.

"Perkins," he replied. "I like their omelets."

*Oh, boy*, I thought. *I get to watch Hardrock eat eggs.*


TO BE HONEST, I was glad to have the sale of the Gettysburg Avenue property behind me. I could go back to my normal life, my normal wife, and my normal routine, or so I believed at the time. But despite being removed from Iris physically, she was never far from my mind.

I'd be delivering my salesman patter to some yuppie couple or blue-collar types, and, for a split second, Iris would be in the room with us, watching from behind her dark veil. Or I'd be walking with Mavis when the hand I held became Iris' marvelous, misshapen claw. Mowing the lawn became an opportunity to dwell in a fantasy realm where Iris was my muse and all the world revolved around her and me.

Then, one afternoon, about a week after closing on the Gettysburg house, I was staring out my office window, in the thralls of an Iris daydream, when my cell phone rang.

I didn't recognize the number, but I have a lot of business cards in circulation. "Yes?"

"I hope I'm not calling at a bad time." It was her! I'd know that tangled speech anywhere.

"Miss Hardrock?" My mouth went dry as the desert sand.

"Yes, I hope this isn't too irregular, calling you back after a sale, but I was wondering if you might be free for lunch sometime this week. I wanted to go over a few items with you while Harold's at work. If you could drop by around noontime?"

"Certainly," I replied without hesitation, surprising myself with my eagerness. I cleared my throat, then consulted my desktop calendar. "Does Friday work for you?"

"Friday will be fine." I could almost hear her smiling over the phone. Then, she thanked me and hung up.

Friday was still two days away, giving trepidation a chance to go to work on me. *Was this really wise? Seeing her alone in her house? A married man? Knowing the effect she had on me?*

Though certain this rendezvous was a mistake, I couldn't bring myself to avoid it. For two days, I remained on edge, fidgety, sweating more than normal.

Mavis would catch me daydreaming during *Wheel of Fortune* or *The Weakest Link* and remark on how absentminded I seemed lately.

"We should take a vacation," she'd say. "Go to Mount Rushmore, the Grand Canyon, or someplace else we've never been. Get away from it all for a while. You've been working too hard."

Though well-meaning, these comments irritated me to no end, but I tried to hide my true feelings, falling back on the pensive-husband cliché, "Yes, dear."

Those two days were agony. When Friday at last rolled around, I was ready to jump out of my skin, I was so nervous. Nervous as a poodle in a veterinarian's office. I was up at daybreak, in the agency an hour early, and spent the morning garrisoned in my office with one eye on the clock.

Promptly at noon, I rapped on the door of the house on Gettysburg Avenue, trying mightily to compose myself. I heard movement inside, recognized the distressed shuffle of my true heart's yearning's approach, and watched as the entrance opened and she, wearing her black veil and a frumpy housecoat, uttered, "Hello. I wasn't sure you'd come. Let me get you some tea."

I noticed at once she was barefoot, and her feet were as deliciously strange as the rest of her body: the toenails overgrown, thick and yellow; the toes themselves displaying painful-looking corns; the phalanges and attached bones badly warped; the heels rough and callused; one inner foot hosting a bunion the size of a baby's fist; and the instep was a glorious medley of angry-blue veins and blotched flesh. The hem of her housecoat also revealed scaley, red ankles and an inch or so of unshaven shins.

It was all I could do to keep from staring in wonder.

The house was largely furnished, though it still lacked the little touches that would give it that lived-in feeling. I took a seat at the kitchen table, which was new and, I guessed, from Ikea or some similar outlet. Two gilded cups and various teas awaited on the table's surface before me.

I watched her fetch the teapot from the stove and marveled at the crude dexterity of her unguiculate hands, though I must admit I was quite relieved when she set the steaming pot down on the table.

"And how are you and Mr. Hardrock enjoying your home?" I asked, picking at a loose thread on the sleeve of my suit jacket—a ruse to delay looking directly at her and risk falling too quickly under her spell.

"The house is fine," she said. "The neighborhood's pleasant. Much better than that rat trap where Harold had us living in Detroit." I felt her eyes on me through the veil.

Adopting my bravest poker face, I glanced her way and asked, "How can I help you, Miss Hardrock?"

"Call me Iris. Please. Surely, we know each other well enough to be on a first-name basis."

When I reached for my teacup, my elbow slipped on the table. I felt myself color. I must've looked like a complete imbecile. I paused, cleared my throat again, and said gently, "How can I help you, *Iris*?"

She somewhat shakily splashed hot water into her cup, chose a Twinings oolong teabag, and dipped it until the water took on a rich hue. More of a coffee man myself, I cluelessly pondered the variety of teas displayed on the table. Ultimately, I followed her lead and also selected the oolong, poured the water, and set about steeping the teabag.

31

"What you could do for me"—and here she inserted my first name, which had never before sounded as grand, spoken by anyone else's lips (even if she did slur it a tad)—"may be a little outside your venue. It's something more of a *personal* nature."

A bead of sweat popped on my forehead. "Yes, anything, you name it!" I wanted to respond. But, of course, I didn't, instead offering a more subdued, "If I can help, I will."

She contemplated the steam rising from her cup. "As I'm sure you've noticed, Uncle Harold makes most of my decisions for me. This is not the way I'd prefer things to be." The last few words ran together, and it took me a moment to understand what she was saying.

"I see," I said at last.

"I'm perfectly capable of making my own choices. I may be *disadvantaged* in some respects, but my mind is sharp. And, these days, food and other essentials are a phone call away. And most business can be readily conducted over the computer. I could hire someone to do the chores I find difficult. I could live quite contently without Harold's meddling in my affairs."

She lifted the cup to her chin, then hesitated. "I would think someone in your line of work would know *attorneys*."

Ah! That was it. That's what she wanted. To help her find a way to get legally free of Hardrock. In some ways, I felt dashed that she'd contacted me for such a utilitarian purpose. But she at least considered me an ally. That buoyed me some.

She set down her cup and leaned toward me. "As long as we're being candid," she said, speaking as if her lips had gone numb, "I want to take off my veil, but I won't if you don't want me to."

"Want you to?"

"I should warn you that my appearance can be somewhat … *disquieting*. I was born this way, you see. I have a rare genetic fault, complicated by my mother's addiction to opioids and psychedelics throughout her pregnancy. It's a marvel really that the doctors managed to keep me alive at all. I was in the hospital for months, and my condition was, as they say, touch and go. But, bucking the odds, I survived. Still, I seldom circulate amongst normal people, and when I do, I always wear the veil. My greatest fear is that someone will look at

32

me and become so shocked they'll have a heart attack. But it's uncomfortable, especially indoors, and poses a difficulty when it comes to drinking anything."

"Nonsense," I said, barely containing my glee. "Of course, you can remove the veil. Pay me no mind."

When she lifted the veil, my eyes met a mottled mass of folded and twisted skin. One of her eyes drooped lower than the other and was all but buried beneath a thick growth. Her teeth, a jagged cluster, crooked and stained, under-bit her upper lip to such a degree that it gave the appearance of her face being sucked into her slanted slash of a mouth. Her hair and eyebrows bristled out angrily in all directions. Her nose resembled a great, rotting pear.

And, yet, the overall effect put me in a trance. Her countenance positively thrilled me.

"My mother died in childbirth," she said. "My heartbroken father died shortly after of a drug overdose. My grandfather took charge of me then, and he doted on me like I meant the world to him, but by the time I was ten years old, he was in his eighties and taking care of me proved beyond his ability. As a child, I needed assistance with my regimen of medicines and to do the most regular things. Eating, getting into bed, going to the bathroom. I've more or less mastered these routines since. But back then, when Grandfather threw in the towel, so to speak, I thought I'd end up in some faceless care facility, which I was not looking forward to. That's when Harold came into the picture."

"He hardly seems the Florence Nightingale type."

She smiled, and her unprincipled teeth formed a lopsided smile that bunched her cheeks in tender lumps of ravaged tissue. "Well, Harold's not big on empathy, that's for certain. But looking after me gives him access to my trust-fund payments, and he gets a small stipend from the government. It pads his income. For the past thirty years, if I'm honest, I've only represented dollar signs to him."

"I'm sorry to hear that." And I was sorry, to the point of being heartsick.

I agreed to speak to a lawyer friend of mine, (not the one who represented me in court, but a commercial attorney who was a former classmate of mine at Cooper High School). We finished our tea, she

33

thanked me, I lightly touched one of her claws in reassurance, and I left, electrified by having seen her face and by our shared moment of sociability.

I DIDN'T GO BACK TO WORK. How could I? Instead, I called Janna at the office and, since I had no showings or other business that day, told her I planned on taking a little holiday. Mavis was at one of her book-club luncheons, so at least I didn't have to account to her for my afternoon presence. It took me all afternoon, pacing in my shuttered den, just to stop my hands from shaking.

Hours passed. I poured myself a generous glassful of Baileys Irish Cream and relived my rendezvous with Iris again and again. What was it about her delightful morbidity that so absorbed me? That made me want to be with her, to caress her puckered flesh, to make love to her discolored gathers, wrinkles, and folds?

When Mavis arrived, I told her I had some prospects to call and some paperwork to finish up and that I'd probably just have Progresso canned soup for supper in the den if that was alright with her.

"Certainly, darling. You run along, and I'll fix you that soup."

My den was upstairs, and the wood flooring outside the room's door featured squeaky boards that alerted me whenever Mavis approached. That was my signal to engage in some real-estate salesmanship theatrics. "Yes, Mr. Blunt, I think I have just the condominium for you. And, yes, they allow pets." "No, Mrs. Morning, the seller is quite firm on the asking price. There are other parties interested in that property." "I don't know if the basement is finished. I'll have to check." And so on, talking blithely into my dial tone.

After she was gone, I returned to my evening's reverie. And this was when my fantasies took a dark turn.

First of all, I've never been an experimentalist in coital matters. With me, it was always the missionary position or, at most, female-superior. I, of course, tried holding back to ensure my partner's satisfaction, but that was about the extent of my playbook. It was enough for Mavis and me, and had been for almost twenty years. But, then again, neither had I ever even fantasized being a philanderer.

Iris coming into my life changed all that. When I imagined erotic situations with her, a wave of the vilest perversity rushed through me.

I imagined myself bound naked to a post, with one of Iris' lobster extremities clutching the butt knot of a braided-leather bullwhip as she laid lash after lash across my bare shoulders and the small of my back. I imagined the shock of the sting, the bruises and welts rising, the trickle of blood from my rent flesh. I fancied her flogging my buttocks and calves and the soles of my feet until the salt of my sweat burned like acid on my skin, and my battered form quit shuddering and hung in limp submission. Endless tears dripped from my chin. I became her spent and pathetic puppet.

Or I'd be lying on my back, pegged to the grass and once again naked, squirming in the heat of the sun. She'd kick at me viciously with her pointy stilettos, landing wicked blows on my legs and sides. Where she struck me, purple and green patches bloomed on my skin. A rib cracked. A boot to the side of my face had my head swimming and my ear throbbing, but I welcomed the pain, in fact, relished it. Then she walked on my chest, on my neck, on my cheek, and ground in her heels, and I begged her with every step to press harder still.

This imagery excited yet confused me. I was never a masochist, nor had I ever been interested in becoming one. Who was this shadowy flagellant who represented me in these visions?

That night, I went to bed after one in the morning. Mavis slept fitfully. I rolled restlessly in and out of dreams that roiled with hurt and lesions and unleashed rapture, and I realized at daybreak that, whoever I was becoming, I was giving myself wholeheartedly to the transformation.

JANNA ENTERED MY OFFICE, offering fresh coffee, but I'd barely touched my first cupful. Looking into the cold liquid, I noticed a dead fly floating on the surface.

"I don't mean to pester you, but is everything okay?" she asked.

Much as I despised being yanked from a fantasy in midstream, so to speak, I looked up at her from my desk, adopting an air of innocence. "Yes, Janna. Whatever do you mean?"

It was my own fault, really, having over the years adopted a familiarity with her that encouraged such assaults on my privacy.

"You haven't been yourself lately. You seem preoccupied. And I noticed that you canceled a showing for Thursday."

"Rescheduled it for next week."

"Still..."

I acted as if her concerns were silliness. "I assure you, Janna, everything's right as rain."

She studied me intensely from behind her aviator eyeglasses, started to say something else, but then thought better of it.

"Do we have any tea?" I said, changing the subject. "Twinings oolong, by any chance? If not, why don't you take some money from petty cash and run over to Byerly's and get us some. I have a real hankering for Twinings oolong tea today."

"Alright." She wore the expression of someone who'd just been hit in the face with a shovel. Never before had I ever shown a fondness for tea, and I suppose this startled her. Then, without another word, she turned and whisked off.

From my office window, I watched as she left the building and crossed the parking lot to her car.

As soon as she pulled away, I called my attorney friend Jackson Greavor, as I'd promised Iris I would. Jack worked at the Minneapolis law firm, Helmuth and Marley, and besides being an old school lunch chum, we'd both gotten to third base with Nora Klingman at her eleventh-grade birthday party. Strange as it sounds, this gave us a special connection.

"Jackson. How you doing, you old snake?"

"You know, still chasing ambulances and paring verbiage in obtuse documents. Lawyer stuff. And you? Still peddling over-priced hovels to the great unwashed?"

We shared a chuckle, badmouthed the president and each other's spouses and, in Jackson's case, the children he passed off as borderline delinquents. Yes, we agreed that, all things considered, we were both doing adequate-to-well-enough in our chosen professions and lifestyles.

"Listen, my friend, what do you know about guardianship contracts?"

36

I explained Iris' position, and how she felt capable of conducting her affairs without the interference of a meddlesome uncle.

"Well," he said, "the goal of a guardianship is ultimately to restore the rights of the individual. Ideally, these agreements are reassessed yearly and monitored to ensure that situations like your client's don't occur. I'd need to read the contract, of course, but offhand, I'd say Iris stands an excellent chance of kicking her leech of a relative to the curb."

"And what will this cost her?"

"How does a pitcher of Grain Belt and some table time at Two Stooges pool hall sound? With you, of course, not Iris."

"Make that jiggers of Baileys, and you've got a deal. Take care of yourself, Jackson, and I'll get back to you as soon as I get a copy of that contract."

My next call was to Iris to give her the good news. It was now Monday, three days since my visit to Gettysburg Avenue, and it was delicious hearing her voice again, every slurred and run-on syllable of it.

"So, you say there's a contract involved?"

"According to Jackson, you should have a copy, and its terms should be open to annual consideration. When was your last review?"

The phone went silent for a time. Then she said, "Review?"

"You've never had a review, have you?"

"Not that I'm aware of."

"And you've never seen this supposed guardianship contract?"

"I haven't."

My blood went scalding hot. This Hardrock character was clearly bilking her.

"Can you ask him for some proof that he is, indeed, your legal guardian?"

Another pause. "When I've broached the subject in the past, he's turned into a raving lunatic. Threatened to put me in a nursing home and wash his hands of me."

I've never been a violent man, but at the moment, if Hardrock had been with me in my office, I would've been unable to resist clutching that miserable wretch by his throat and squeezing the life out of him. I

37

was so consumed with this idea that I thought I heard a voice say, "Do it!" A woman's voice, familiar yet unidentifiable.

I felt a prickly stab of anxiety. *Get control of yourself, man. You're falling apart. Losing it.*

"No one's putting you in any nursing home, Iris," I said firmly. "I'll see to that. Just give me a day or two to talk with some people and figure out how to proceed on this, with or without Uncle Harold's cooperation."

"Be careful. I wouldn't want him getting wind of any of this."

"Mum's the word," I reassured her. But I wondered how long I could really keep Hardrock out of the loop.

I TALKED WITH OTHER ATTORNEYS, with acquaintances, law enforcement, and social workers, always posing the problem as a theoretical proposition or an inquiry on behalf of a friend. As it turned out, what I was really doing was leaving a trail of bread crumbs for the authorities who'd later come searching for a motive.

But that's getting ahead of the story.

"I wish I had better news," I said to her on Wednesday during our second clandestine meeting at Gettysburg Avenue over oolong tea, "but, if there's no actual guardianship contract, and Uncle Harold has gotten his grubby paws on your money through some kind of subterfuge, then you're in a trickier situation."

"Subterfuge? What do you mean?"

"Let's say he hoodwinked you into signing papers giving him control of your resources."

She thoughtfully scratched her rotting pear of a nose. "Well, now that you mention it, he has had me sign things I wasn't always clear on."

"My guess is he had you sign many things that gave him legal leverage over your affairs."

"Can't I just call the police and get him out of my house?"

"It's not your house, Iris. It's yours and Harold's. Both of your names are on the title. You signed the papers, and Janna notarized them."

A teardrop formed in her drooping eye. "There's nothing I can do?"

"I didn't say that. But you could be facing a lengthy process, and your uncle would know what you're up to, of course."

Her scraggly lower teeth gnawed at her lip. Now both her eyes glistened, and her mottled form rocked in sobs. A stream of drool trickled down her chin. It was the most heartrending sight ever. She mumbled and blathered pitifully.

"Don't lose hope, Iris," I said, clasping one of her fleshy pinchers. "I'll find a way."

"Do it." That voice again, that familiar yet undistinguishable woman's voice, soft and clear. "Do it," the voice insisted. "Kill him."

I froze in terror, looking around the kitchen. Where could that voice have come from? The sink? The stove vent? Maybe from somewhere within the house's walls?

"Did you just hear that?" But Iris was so consumed with the hopelessness of her own situation as to be oblivious to all else.

It didn't matter. In my heart, I secretly knew where the voice was coming from: it came from *inside* my head.


IT WAS ALMOST THREE O'CLOCK when I got back to the agency. Janna handed me a stack of messages and gave me a troubled look, but said nothing. I told her to take the rest of the day off, then I turned out the lights, entered the sanctity of my office, and closed the door.

I stared at the parking lot outside my window and brooded. The appearance of this disembodied voice worried me. Of course, I had no intention of following its edict, but I couldn't help wondering what triggered it.

*Should I see someone? A counselor, maybe, or some other professional?*

And what about these other thoughts that so occupied my mind lately; these reemerging masochistic fantasies about Iris that were draining me of time and productivity, of interest in spending pleasant evenings with Mavis, and of just about anything else that had once seemed important? Aside from these imaginary trysts (if you could even call them that), my whole life seemed suddenly, remarkably otherwise mundane.

Once again, I felt myself slipping into my imaginary world. Iris was beating me woozy and demanding I smell and lick her bare, mangled feet.

The next thing I knew, it was after seven o'clock. The parking lot was all but empty.

I rose from behind my desk, unsteady on my feet. Mavis would be holding dinner for me. I stumbled out the door.

On the drive home, I returned to thoughts of Hardrock and his tyrannical lording over of Iris and her affairs. Once again, the ire swelled within me. The sight of my Iris (yes, I now thought of her as mine) gibbering in despair, feeling trapped in the jaws of fate, replayed in my mind with nightmarish frequency.

At dinner, I saw Mavis' lips moving, stuffed tasteless food in my mouth, nodded and grunted, and *tried* to understand what was going on about me, but my mind was occupied elsewhere. After, I joined my wife on the sofa with a bowl of popcorn and watched a rerun of *Press Your Luck*, but not even Elizabeth Banks, the show's host, looking sharp and fetching in a scarlet pants suit, could pry my interest from Iris and her dilemma.

"Darling, something's been bothering you for days now. What is it?"

*Not this again.* I calmed myself by concentrating on my breathing, in and out, in and out, in the Zen method. "It's nothing. Overworked, I guess."

"You're not hiding anything from me, are you?"

In and out, in and out. "Of course not. What would I be hiding?"

The question hung in the air, unanswered.

During the night, sleep eluded me as thoughts involving Iris raced in my brain. One minute, I confronted Hardrock, demanding he let Iris go. The next, I crawled on hands and knees, dog-like, as Iris led me about on a leash.

On my way to work the next day, red-eyed and groggy, it occurred to me that, perhaps, a present might cheer Iris a bit, so on my lunch hour, I stopped at a shoe store and bought her a pair of ivory sling-back sandals. I had to guess the size, but the salesman assured me I could exchange them if they didn't fit.

At the office, I stashed the boxed shoes in a lower desk drawer, and whenever Janna left to use the bathroom or fill the teapot, I opened the drawer, lifted the lid on the box, and remarked in my mind what a handsome pair of shoes they were. Open-toed, stylish; Italian leather with faux cork heels, and adjustable straps. I took one out and sniffed it, and a flush of excitement lifted me.

That afternoon, I rushed through a showing of a two-bedroom, two-bath Eagan townhouse with a wood-burning fireplace, tongue-and-groove hardwood floors, and a cedar deck that overlooked a scenic pond. Almost twelve-hundred square feet. I might've bought it myself as a spec home if the seller had been willing to come down on the price.

The young couple who saw it were interested but didn't commit. I gave them my card and hurried back to the office.

Fatigue, spent emotions, and fantasy kept me weaving in and out of reality, taking an even steeper toll on me than I realized. After Janna left for the day, I poured myself some oolong tea, extinguished the lights, and retired to my office for an hour or so alone with the shoes. I imagined Iris' feet in the ivory leather, dabbed my tongue to the instep.

Swept away by illusions, fond and abhorrent, one hour turned to two then three. It was after eight when the spell was broken by the peal of my cell phone.

"Where *are* you?" Mavis' voice raged in my ear.

"I'm leaving now," I said thickly. "I'll explain later."

I clicked off the phone and was returning it to my pocket when it rang again. The caller ID said Mavis.

Still in a daze, I answered, a new lie taking shape in my mouth. "I'm sorry. I must have dozed off…"

Here I was interrupted, not by Mavis' voice, but by another familiar one: "Do it now. Kill him." And the line went dead.

THE ONLY WAY I COULD SEE TO CLEAR UP THIS MESS was—with or without Iris' permission—to confront Hardrock directly. If he balked at freeing her out of the goodness of his heart, perhaps a deal could be made, a payoff of some kind. Speak to the man, find wiggle room. Didn't I negotiate with buyers and sellers for a living? Surely, I could find common ground with this miscreant.

41

It was worth a try. Despite the counsel of my disembodied adviser, I had no intention of killing anyone.

As luck would have it, the previous owners of the property on Gettysburg Avenue had dropped off some spare keys at the agency. The seller wasn't sure what all of them were for, but one was to a side door in the garage, and one might have been to a neighbor's house. This kind of thing happens often in the real-estate business. It comes under the heading of loose ends. Typically, a situation like this would be remedied quickly and cleanly through the U.S. mail, but this time, I thought, I'd deliver the keys personally, when I was reasonably certain Hardrock would be home.

I spent the next day envisioning how Hardrock might react to various approaches. I fleshed out imagined parleys, arguments, and objections; constructed foolproof rejoinders; and, overall, devised intricate frameworks of logic in which to ensnare the fiend.

The following day was Saturday. Usually, I'd schedule several showings or an open house on a Saturday, out of consideration for my largely working-class clientele, but this day, I left my schedule blank, though I had Janna double-up my Sunday showings. I wasn't sure how my discussion with Hardrock would go, and I figured I might need flexibility in my timetable. Frankly, the thought of discussing Iris with him left me unnerved.

When I pulled up, Hardrock was stepping into the driveway from his open garage, holding a rusty, single-bladed fire axe. At first, he didn't recognize me. "Are you looking for something?"

"Remember me? I'm your realtor. I sold you this house."

He turned his head to one side and gave me a look of disbelief, and I didn't like the way he was holding that axe. Then he seemed to relax, and the axe lowered. "Is there a problem?"

"No. Nothing like that." I groped the keyring from my pocket and held it out. "Previous owner dropped these off. Said they were spares."

"Alright." He reached out and took them from me. "Did he say what they were for?"

As I related what the seller had told me, I noticed Iris watching us from beyond a linen curtain. She was veilless, and her lopsided eyes

42

viewed me with trepidation. I smiled at her and nodded reassuringly as Hardrock studied the keys.

"Alright," he said again. "Is that all then?" He meant to dismiss me.

"Actually, I was hoping we might talk about something else."

He looked at me as if I was a panhandler begging change. Finally, he said with skepticism, "Alright. But I have some work to do out back. You'll have to do your talking while I chop down a dead tree." He held up the axe.

"Of course," I said, following him.

In the corner of the yard, one of the trees had gone dead: an ash tree claimed, no doubt, by the emerald borers that had plagued half of New Hope in recent years. The beetles lay their eggs in a tree's bark, and their offspring feed on the wood for two years before emerging and repeating the cycle.

We approached the defunct ash, which was only about ten feet tall so could feasibly be cut down without endangering the garage or any nearby neighbors' buildings. Hardrock rolled up his sleeves and gripped the axe handle with both hands.

"Thought I'd try out that fireplace. Burn a log or two and see if the flue needs cleaning." He pulled back and swung the rusty metal blade like Harmon Killebrew leaning into a fastball. The contact made a hacking sound and sprayed bark into the lawn. He stepped back and inspected the damage the blow had left on the tree trunk. Then he added, "This is about Iris, isn't it?"

A thousand thoughts flooded in, leaving me stunned and speechless.

Before I could answer, Hardrock swung the axe again, putting all he had into it. The blade sliced in deeper; deep enough that he had to rock it back and forth to free it from the ash's grip. He turned to me, wearing a smug expression. "It's happened before. In Detroit, Chicago, and before that, Milwaukee—that's where our people are from originally. What draws you perverts to her, I've no idea. The first time, it was a mail carrier. Bill something or other. The last time, it was a handyman named Oswald who solicited work by going door-to-door. Pudgy little fellow. Greasy hair. Swearing out a restraining order drove off Bill, but not Oswald. I finally had to chase him off physically with this axe." He stroked the handle lovingly. "And I left him with a reminder not to come back. Poor idiot walks with a limp now."

He took a menacing step toward me. "I've got to hand it to Iris. Once she gets her hooks into someone, she gets them in good."

I struggled to maintain my equilibrium. "But if she brings you so much trouble, why not just let her go?"

"Let my cash cow go? Unlikely. I make more money off the endowments her father left her than I make at 3M. The life-insurance policy alone paid for this house, and could pay for a dozen more. With Iris, I'm a wealthy man. Without her, I'm just another working schlub."

"Why hasn't anyone reported you to the police?"

"One tried it. Wonder whatever happened to that guy? I heard he just disappeared." Hardrock's eyes glinted meaningfully. He took another step closer.

Just then, a neighbor approached from across the facing backyard of an adjacent property. A grizzled, sixtyish geezer with thick eyeglasses, teeth too white to be real, and a forward hunch. "Hey, neighbor," he said amiably. "I hate to interrupt, but we haven't met yet."

Hardrock turned to the greeter, and I dove for the axe handle. I yanked, and he yanked, and eventually, I tore from his hands.

"Hey," the neighbor said, uncertain of what was going on.

In that instant, all my awareness imploded in a brilliant crimson flash. A clattering sound filled my ears, like a drawerful of knives crashing to the floor. The fabric of reality peeled away, baring a kaleidoscope of images, run through with flames of hatred and dim outlines of shadowy creatures on spindlelegs. The taste of smoke filled my lungs. I pictured Hardrock attacking me with the axe; Iris dressed as a dominatrix, cracking her whip and snapping her protruding lower jaw at me; Janna asking me, again and again, if I was alright; Mavis eyeing me as if ashamed of me. And that voice again, demanding that I "kill him, KILL him, KILL HIM!"

Caught in that wave of hallucination, I'm not sure how I found the strength to lift the axe. My arms grew deadened; my hands seemed no longer connected to me. A cold sweat washed over my body, and, lightheaded, I slipped toward the brink of laughter. Maybe I *was* laughing. I'm not sure.

44

Through it all, I remember Hardrock's narrow face: first twisted in anger, then flushed with terror, then white as a sunlit snowdrift. The shadow of the axe crossed his forehead. The handle shivered in my hands as the blade sank solidly into his skull, and the first gush of his blood splashed hot and viscous on my cheek. I swung the axe again, splattering myself and the thunderstruck neighbor. And again, I swung.

Hardrock collapsed to the ground.

I turned to the blood-bespattered neighbor, who stood gaping at me, trembling.

Before he could say anything, I raised the axe and brought it down on the crown of his head, the bloodlust swirling inside me like a swarm of hornets. He looked at me like he couldn't believe what I'd just done. I couldn't believe it either. Nor could I when the axe chopped down again on the nape of his neck, and the side of his head, lopping off an ear.

He tumbled to the grass beside Hardrock, and I paused for an instant as all the world stood still.

Then I turned back toward the house. Iris was at the window watching, horrified, speaking excitedly into a cell phone.

I could have run, but what was the use? Instead, I sat on the lawn beside the two men I'd just killed. I threw aside the axe and, shuddering alternately with sobs and laughter, waited for the police to arrive.

SHE APPEARED IN THE WITNESS BOX, wearing her black veil, and tearfully recounted the deaths of her uncle and her neighbor. Her voice was so slurred and shaky, the prosecuting attorney had to ask her several times to repeat herself. It never occurred to me that she would be saddened by Hardrock's demise, not given the distress he'd caused her all those years. But who can explain the workings of the human heart?

She was at least free of his yoke, whether she thanked me for it or not.

I heard from my attorney that she stayed in the house on Gettysburg, living as a recluse. A hired caregiver came to her house once a week, and delivery people brought her essentials. I wrote to her regularly, but she never wrote back. I hope she read at least some of the letters, but I'm not fooling myself.

After the verdict, Mavis divorced me, of course, and took sole possession of all our funds and property. The agency closed, and Janna took a job as an administrative assistant at Helmuth and Marley, the law firm where my school bud Jackson worked. Small world.

My Iris may be lost to me physically, but I still have my imaginings: endless hours of my grotesque mistress, biting, lashing me, pulling my hair. And me, her willing slave, underfoot, writhing in ecstasy. If I didn't have to eat, to sleep, to exercise my hour a day, or to listen to my cellmate Bobby's tiresome tale of woe, I could be with her always. That's all I really want.

"… the gun went off, and he was on the floor, staring back at me, lifeless," Bobby said for the umpteenth time as the dinner hour approached.

I listened to Bobby, to the clang of the barred doors opening and feet shuffling in the corridors, and, as we climbed from our cots, something else caught my ear: a faint utterance that whispered to me from the darkest labyrinth of my conscience. "Do it," the voice said.

I looked at Bobby and said, "After you, my friend."

# THE PORTER

"The veneer of civilization vanished. Naked but for loin-cloth and
girded sword he strode across the plain, carrying the golden cask
under his arm."
—Robert E. Howard, "The House of Arabu"

**H**ey, kid. Want to make some easy money?"

The voice came from a car parked on the side of the
road: a shiny new Dodge Intrepid, rainy gray with sixteen-
inch touring tires. Trevor Bates, seventeen, walked to the
car and leaned into the open passenger-side window.

"Were you talking to me?" he asked.

The woman, who looked to be in her mid-twenties, was a knockout:
strawberry blonde with blue eyes that she wasn't shy about batting at
him. She wore a loose-fitting cotton blouse that gave her body room to
move in and jean shorts that displayed ample leg. A smile played at her
lips. "Of course, I'm talking to you, dear boy. Did you think I was
talking to myself?"

Trevor, who was heading home from a morning of shooting hoops
with a few friends, carried himself with the prowess and confidence of
an athlete but without the arrogance so many of them tend to show;
though, if anyone deserved to be full of himself, it was Trevor. His
talents as a shooting guard for the Cooper High School Hawks
basketball team had recently earned him a full-ride scholarship to
Mankato State University.

He looked up and down the sidewalks of Winnetka Avenue, at
distant straggling pedestrians, and weighed his words. "Out of the blue,
you're offering me a job?"

"That's right."

"What kind of job?"

"I need a porter."

"A what?"

"A porter. Someone to carry boxes for me."

He eyed her doubtfully. "What kind of boxes?"

She leaned across the seat toward him, giving him a healthy survey of cleavage. "What difference does it make?"

"You stop me on the street and ask me to move some mysterious boxes for you, and I'm not supposed to be suspicious?"

"I'll pay you a hundred bucks. Half up front."

He rubbed his chin. "How long will it take?"

"As long as it takes. Not long."

"This isn't about drugs or anything like that, is it? I don't want to get into any trouble."

"You won't. Trust me. Hop in."

She looked harmless enough.

He thought about it a second, then shrugged. "Okay," he said, opening the door. "But if I'm not comfortable at any time, I'm walking away."

She handed him fifty dollars, he climbed in, and the Intrepid angled away from the curb into traffic.

It was a warm and sunny late-summer afternoon. A bruiser with a thick, bull neck in a muscle shirt pushed a sputtering lawn mower across a yard. An old woman in a sombrero sat in a picnic chair, sipping a cold drink, and watched them drive past. Some neighborhood kids played hopscotch on the sidewalk. Just a typical Saturday afternoon in New Hope, Minnesota.

"You in high school, dear boy?" she asked.

"Trevor. My name's Trevor." That "dear boy" stuff was starting to get to him.

"And I'm Sam. You in high school, Trevor?"

"A senior at Cooper."

"Have a girlfriend?"

"Not exactly."

"In between, huh?"

He shrugged.

First stop was a liquor store in nearby Golden Valley. She bought a case of Chevas Regal and a couple of twelve-packs of Moosehead beer. She knew the guy working behind the counter, called him by name—Reggie—and they talked while Trevor carried out the booze. When he came back inside, a corded wooden box, looking like some relic from a pirate ship, waited on the counter for him.

Reggie watched solemnly, eyes collared in dark wrinkles, as Trevor lifted the box.

Whatever it was, it was heavy.

"This it?" Trevor asked.

"That's it for this stop," Sam said. "See you later, Reggie."

As Trevor loaded the box into the back seat, he couldn't help asking, "What's in that box, anyway?"

"Oh, this and that," came the response.

They climbed back into the Intrepid and Sam headed south on Highway 100.

St. Louis Park, best known as the birthplace of movie directors, Joel and Ethan Coen, lies just west of Minneapolis. Incorporated in eighteen-eighty-six, the city got its name from the Minneapolis and St. Louis Railway that ran through it. Its population skews toward Russians and Jews, and homes there tend to be fairly upscale.

Sam pulled off the highway and soon had them cruising through a shady, residential area on St. Louis Park's southeast side, near Dakota Park. She pulled up in front of a beige two-story, brick-and-shingle New England-style home, maybe fifty years old. A white concrete walkway led them to a glass outer door. The inner door was paneled in stylish walnut.

Sam rang the bell.

The door opened, and in the threshold stood a plump, hunched geezer, eighty or ninety years old, clutching a black cane in one hand. He had a head of tousled white hair, fine as spider silk, and running down one side of his wrinkled face were an array of age spots the color of root beer. He wore a red velvet robe with black lapels that resembled an old-fashioned smoking jacket.

When his eyes fell on Sam, his whole face lit up. "Sam! I was wondering when I'd see you again." Then he turned toward Trevor and asked her warily, "Who's your friend?"

His eyes weren't rheumy or dull in the way a lot of old people's eyes are, but were sharp and focused on Trevor as if expecting at any moment a treacherous move.

"Arthur, this is Trevor. He's my porter today." She turned to Trevor, squinted, and raised one eyebrow in an expression he couldn't decipher. "Trevor, this is Arthur."

She faced the old man again. Arthur and Trevor nodded to one another.

"Your package is out back. But let me get a box first, so I can send you home with some tomatoes and cucumbers from the garden."

He vanished inside and reemerged minutes later with an empty Xerox copy-paper box. He handed the box to Trevor, then led them around the side of the house. They entered the backyard through the gate of a tall privacy fence.

Arthur tapped his cane in the grass as he ambled along, not using it as a walking aid at all. He led them to a large vegetable garden, freshly watered and weeded. Moving down the neat rows, he inspected and plucked vegetables from assorted leafy plants: tomatoes, cucumbers, squash, cauliflower, cabbage. He handed these to Sam, who dropped them in the Xerox box. When the box was about three-quarters full, Arthur rubbed the dirt from his hands and Sam thanked him for the veggies.

Then they headed toward a gabled wooden shed, the hunched old-timer tapping his cane as he walked arm-in-arm with Sam. The shed was ten feet by eight with an eight-foot peaked ceiling. It had a shingled roof and two wide doors joined at a swiveled hasp, secured with an industrial padlock. From the pocket of his smoking-jacket robe Arthur pulled a bunch of keys, ferreted out the correct one, and unlocked the shed. The doors opened silently.

Inside hunkered a Craftsman riding lawnmower that looked more like a tractor, and a gas-powered snow blower with an enormous intake shovel. Situated between them lay a shiny, lavender-colored box, oblong and tapered. It was about four feet long and six inches at its widest, and inset on its top was a working compass.

Trevor set down the vegetables and hefted the container. It weighed about fifty pounds, and when he lugged it into the daylight, the sun glared back from its shiny surface as if it were mirrored. All three of them turned their faces from the brightness.

"I'll take this out to the car and come back for the vegetables," Trevor said.

"You'll want to put that in the trunk," Sam said, handing him the keys.

When he came back, Arthur was sliding a handful of cash into his wallet.

"What's that box made out of anyway?" Trevor asked.

Sam and Arthur looked at each other and laughed. Trevor picked up the vegetable box, feeling his face redden.

"Let me show you something, son," the hunched old man said, a wide grin (probably dentures) parted his spotted, wrinkled face. "You've probably been wondering why I'm carrying this cane but not really using it to walk."

He held out the cane in two open hands for Trevor to examine.

The cane was a little over three feet long, round, and made of wood with a midnight black finish. It had an intricately cast, black-steel pommel and a runnel-grip handle.

"I take this with me everywhere. Never leave the house without it. I don't need it to walk, but it still comes in handy sometimes. Watch and learn."

Arthur grabbed the cane by its handle, clicked a mechanism, and the wooden shaft slid away and fell to the ground, revealing two feet of double-edged metal blade. He held the tip of the blade two inches from Trevor's nose. "That's twenty-four inches of razor-sharp Damascus steel. The hilt and fittings are heavy cast metal. What do you think?"

Trevor stepped back with the box of vegetables in his arms. "That's c-cool," he said, shakily.

"The lesson to be learned is, things aren't always what they appear to be." Arthur lowered the sword, bent over, and picked up the discarded wooden shaft. He slid it back on and it locked into place. "Also," Arthur added, tapping the grass with it, "be careful who you tangle with. You never know what may be up their sleeves."

Trevor wasn't sure how any of this addressed his question about the box, but decided to let the matter drop.

"We done yet?" Trevor asked, as they approached the ramp to Highway 7.

"Not quite."

"You said it wouldn't take very long."

"I said it would take as long as it takes." She glanced at him with those baby-blues, and he felt his resistance melting. "Two more stops, then it's home again, home again, jiggity jig."

Well, come to think of it, this was—so far, anyway—the easiest hundred bucks Trevor had ever made. He contented himself with watching traffic out the window as they headed west.

The next stop on their merry adventure was Hopkins, a semi-charming burg of about four square miles with a quaint downtown main street. First settled in eighteen-fifty-two, the town was originally known as West Minneapolis, but was later renamed after Henry H. Hopkins, the city's first postmaster. These days, Hopkins is a community of affordable homes and low crime. To the outside world, it's known almost exclusively for its Raspberry Festival, which dates back to the days of the Great Depression.

They walked into one of the downtown antique stores and headed toward the back. The shop featured tall glass cases full of worn toys, coins, tools, baseball cards, dishes, clothing and every other possible kind of memorabilia Trevor could imagine. There was furniture for sale and shelves full of books and record albums. In the back, they went through a door labeled EMPLOYEES ONLY, then through a small storage room to a curtained entryway that led to downward stairs.

At the foot of the stairs was another door, on which Sam rapped some kind of coded knock. The door unlocked and opened, and standing in a bricked threshold was a bitter-faced, middle-aged woman in teardrop eyeglasses stroking a black cat. The woman wore teal lipstick and matching eye shadow, and a lot of lacey black.

She nodded to Sam, greeting her with, "Blessed be."

As far as Trevor was concerned, he might've been invisible, but Sam introduced him anyway. "Trevor, this is Grian. Grian, Trevor."

He offered his hand but she ignored it.

The inside room was pretty much what you'd expect an unfinished basement to be: lots of cemetery-gray cement cracked in spots, framed stud walls leaking pink insulation, and naked light bulbs suspended from the ceiling. Long tables, most of them empty, fed out from the far wall. The closest table was stacked with candles, crystals, dried herbs in corked vials, and a U.S. Army footlocker that looked like a prop from *Saving Private Ryan*.

In the near corner was what Trevor took to be an altar, though not of any religion he was familiar with. Flames sizzled in jeweled candleholders before resin statues of goat-headed gods. One shelf held dim brass and dull silver pentagrams, a smoking incense burner and—most unsettling—photographs of people with their eyes crossed out.

"Nice cat," Trevor said, breaking the silence.

"I found him sitting on a grave one afternoon at Grandview Park. Sitting and waiting for me." Grian didn't exactly smile but she flashed a sliver of teeth. "Cats and birds are drawn to graves that are active. This grave was an old one. Benjamin Bronski, died nineteen-o-one. His gravestone was fractured and worn. I kept a splinter of it. No rest for Benjamin, apparently. Anyway, Mr. Frizzy followed me home, and he's been with me ever since."

Grian set the cat down on the floor and went to the nearby table.

"These are the candles you wanted," Grian said to Sam. "Made in Romania of genuine wolf fat. And this incense comes from a monastery in Tibet. Very hard to get."

Mr. Frizzy padded over to Trevor and rubbed himself against his ankle, but when Trevor bent to pet the cat, he hissed at him and scurried off toward the altar. Mr. Frizzy lay down in front of it, stretched and purred.

"Trevor, why don't you take this out to the car," Sam said, drumming her fingers on the footlocker.

Getting it up the stairs was awkward. Since he didn't know the contents, he wasn't sure how much jostling they could take, but he tried to be careful with the container. It wasn't overly heavy, but it was clumsy to carry because one end of it was heavier than the other.

When he returned to the back room, Sam was coming up the stairs. She handed him the candles and a musty box of incense, just as the basement door closed and audibly locked behind her.

Their fourth and final pickup spot lay to the north, on Highway 494. Plymouth, the third-largest suburb of Minneapolis, was originally known as Medicine Lake back when it was home to the Dakota tribe, sometime between fourteen- and fifteen-hundred CE. By eighteen-fifty-two, the white man began muscling in on the territory and, by eighteen-eighty, had pretty much taken it over. Plymouth was the one-time home of a number of politicians, several pro athletes, and chess grandmaster Andrew Tang.

They stopped at a grocery store where Sam bought coriander, tarragon, sassafras, and other herbs; capers preserved in vinegar; pistachios, walnuts, filberts, almonds; pomegranates, pineapples, and other fruits; and a gaggle of confectioneries, sweetly frosted and powdered in sugar.

At the deli station, a beefy Black woman in a stained apron fetched from under the counter a lacquered, black box, four inches square and carved in cryptic images. One side panel featured an alligator wearing a tiny hat. Another showed the likeness of a spider with monstrous fangs and many-jointed legs that seemed to grope out at Trevor, as if preparing to strike.

Sam laid the box in the cart's front basket, nodded to the deli worker, and rolled away.

By the time Trevor loaded the bags containing the groceries into the car, the back seat overflowed. Sam set the carved box on the seat between them. On the top of the box, a squid-like woman lurched from a tangle of seaweeds, her tentacles fanned out around her in a demonic nimbus

Eying the box uneasily, he said, "And that's the last pickup?"

"That's the last pickup, Trevor." Sam glanced his way, smiling. "Now, all you've got to do is unload the car, then I'll pay you the rest of your money and cut you free. That is, if you want to be cut free."

That final phrase dripped with innuendo of some kind, but he was afraid to ask what she meant by it.

They drove back to New Hope, followed Bass Lake Road to Boone, turned south, and soon were headed west on Aldinach Trail, a short, winding road lined with poplars and birch trees that ended in a cul-de-sac. Aldinach Trail was unpopulated except for an imposing sandstone manor that overlooked the road's dead end. Towers with decorative railings rose at each corner of the manor, and high, stained glass windows peered down at the travelers from either side of the main doors.

The Intrepid pulled into a driveway of knobby cobblestones, the attached garage opened, and Sam parked inside.

Trevor had grown up in New Hope his whole life and knew his way around town pretty well, but he'd never heard of Aldinach Trail, nor had he the slightest familiarity with this house, which was odd considering its unique structure and placement. Surely someone would have taken more than a passing interest in the manor and mentioned it, especially in this age of blooming social media.

"You live here?" Trevor asked, opening the passenger side door.

Noises from the house carried out to the garage: conversation, laughter, and wild, loopy music with flutes and synthesizers and ... *accordions*? The music was coming from unseen speakers.

"I do live here," Sam said, climbing out of the Intrepid. "Many of us do. Others are our guests. You'll see."

Grabbing an armful of groceries from the back seat, Trevor followed her inside to a tile landing with stairs running up and down. In the center of the landing, a mosaic depiction of the tentacled sea creature he'd seen on the lacquered box pitched up at them from watery depths, seductive and malevolent, with ringed fingers, floating hair, and amphibious eyes. Her tentacles seemed to writhe at him.

Over the main entrance was a sign with letters of gold that read: "Those who speak of things that do not concern them shall hear things that will not please them."

He was about to ask Sam what that meant, when someone called down to them from the head of the stairs.

"Hey, Sam. Hope you don't mind us starting the party without you. Who's your friend?" She spoke full-throated to be heard over the din behind her.

The speaker's voice was booming and gruff, though the speaker herself was barely three feet tall. She reminded him of a gnome in a storybook his mother used to read to him when he was just a toddler. Round and squat, with her hair cut very short, the diminutive woman wore heavy makeup and a frock adorned with a pattern of swimming fish, and she appeared to be dusted in glitter. She toasted them with a glass chalice containing an effervescent liquid.

"Trevor, this is Magog. Trevor here's my porter today."

Sam motioned for Trevor to head up the stairs with the groceries.

Magog stepped back as they passed into a large reception room with maybe two dozen women milling about. Most held drinks and swayed to the rhythm of the music, which sped up and slowed down abruptly, and featured a shrill flute that followed its own course entirely.

"What is this music?" Trevor asked loudly.

Sam looked at him in wonder, as if he'd just said something that made no sense. "Why, it's 'Pan in the Hall of the Mountain King,' of course. Don't tell me you haven't heard it before?"

Trevor shrugged.

A woman with a silky ponytail twirled past him in dance like some heavenly dervish, leaving a trail of lavender-scented perfume in her wake. A skeletal, black-toothed crone with scabby elbows stumbled toward them, clutching a bottle of wine to her chest. Across the room, naked to their waists, three iron-masked women held eel-shaped scepters. Their masks bore twisted imagery with misplaced features and jagged-toothed sneers. Trevor couldn't help staring at their breasts.

If Sam was taken aback by any of this, it didn't show on her expression. "The kitchen's this way," she said, smiling back at him.

They wound past a pair of willowy women—girls really, not much older than Trevor—with silver-white skin contoured in the palest of pink, their eyes amber, their long necks circumscribed in metal collars. The girls conversed with a tall, hawk-faced woman with a shiny bald head and elongated hands and feet. The bald woman's fingernails hung clear to the floor, and her clothing appeared shrouded in gossamer spider webs.

"Wh-who are these people?" Trevor asked.

"People you needn't speak of," Sam replied.

The kitchen lay through an arched entryway bordered in faux brick.

As they crossed through it, their progress drew the attention of a viewer in a hooded, mauve robe that loosely wrapped a generous bosom and apple-shaped body. She appeared serene inside her cowl, her face pleasant and round-cheeked and framed in soft strands of dark, frizzy hair, her eyes a hypnotic azure. Trevor had to force himself to unmeet her gaze.

Sam motioned to a table in the kitchen. "Bring the rest of the groceries here. I'll show you where to put the other boxes." She suggestively tilted her blonde head downward and to one side. He tried to read her blue eyes, but they just shined back at him, enigmatically.

Once the groceries and the cardboard carton of garden vegetables were in, Trevor scooped up the corded, wooden pirate box he'd carried from the liquor store and followed Sam, this time down the stairs to a darkened basement.

She flipped on recessed lights that revealed a large, carpeted, high-ceilinged room, empty of people or furniture but occupied by what Trevor took to be a modern sculpture of some kind. One of the strangest assemblages he'd ever seen.

At its heart, a metal bean, silver and roughly the size of a Volkswagen Beetle, rose about two feet from the floor on jointed wooden legs. The bean sprouted all manner of limbs and appendages made of differing materials in differing dimensions: some mirrored, some crystal, some fashioned from bent copper, others from spun pink glass or cubed glass rods. Cables draped one portion of the bean, while vacuum tubes like old-fashioned radio components lined the top of it, and black dials clustered in a small section left clear. Wires held together with electrical tape hung in loops from metal pegs.

In front of the contraption, in a row, sat six jars containing bonelike masses suspended in an oily liquid that had separated into layers.

"You can bring the rest of the boxes down here," Sam said. "Just lay them to the side. Then, I'll give you the rest of your money and you're free to go."

"What *is* that thing?"

"A thing you don't need to speak of."

Trevor swallowed. "Speak of? I don't even know what I could say about it."

"Good," she said, heading back to the stairs. "Now set down that box and come on."

He carried down the shiny, oblong lavender-colored box with its working compass; the footlocker, candles, and incense collected from the basement of the antique store; and the black lacquered box carved in cryptic images. These he set to one side as instructed, and stood studying the bean and all its accessories. "Is it some kind of machine?"

Sam ignored the question. She handed over the fifty dollars he had coming to him. "You're free to go now." She raised her eyebrows. "Or you could stick around for a while. Maybe get answers to some of your questions."

"Nah. I better get going. It's getting late and my parents will be worried."

"Can you get back on your own, or do you need a ride?"

He stuffed the money into his pocket. "I can walk from here. I don't know this street, but I know Boone and Bass Lake Road. See you around, Sam. Let me know if you ever need someone to lug boxes around for you again."

She put an arm around his shoulder and led him up the steps to the landing with its tiled, tentacled monster woman and the front door. From the living room, Magog raised her glass to him again.

"If you're sure you can't stay," she said, kissing him on the cheek. "Goodbye, Trevor. Enjoy the rest of your life."

He tried to say something, but he was too flustered from her kiss. He felt the blood rush to his face and a tingling sensation in his midsection.

He stepped clumsily through the door, across the yard, into the cul-de-sac, and onto Aldinach Trail. He walked the winding, tree-lined road, then suddenly stopped midstride.

It wasn't really *that* late. The sun was low in the sky but still gave the early evening a golden glow. Sam had clearly wanted him to stay.

*What am I walking away from?* he wondered.

He turned and faced the house, his imagination unspooling an orgiastic vision of Sam and the bare-chested women in the iron masks caressing him. *Okay, maybe that was farfetched, but there was certainly something more than an innocent party going on back there. And what was that contraption in the basement, anyway?*

He decided to sneak back for another look.

Keeping to the trees, he worked his way to the sandstone manor with its colored-glass windows and cobblestone driveway. As he neared the house, the gathering's bizarre music became audible: now jarring from the hidden speakers, a staccato of violins ringing over a chorus of dronepipes, harmonicas, and flugelhorns. He went around the side of the building and lay in the grass to peer into the basement through a clear panel in a ground-level, stained glass depiction of end-days devils roaming a blighted Earth.

Inside, the partygoers assembled around the bean-shaped machine. Their conversations were muffled somewhat but faintly discernible, even over the panoramic piping of the music.

Sam, now wearing a pinguid, green robe and a mitered hat, walked around the device lighting candles and cones of incense, while several of the women added to the contraption the contents of the boxes Trevor had collected.

From the pirate box, the willowy women with the amber eyes plucked a pair of brass objects that resembled grooved rolling pins. These they fitted into depressions on either end of the bean. Next, they removed from the box several foil-like strips, which they attached to the bent copper appendages that protruded out at various angles from the bean. The box itself was folded flat, then slid off to the side.

Sam, still somehow looking gorgeous in her oily robe and Pope hat, picked up the black lacquered cube and held it loosely as she walked among the assemblers, giving them helpful instructions.

Diminutive Magog now began disassembling the oblong lavender-colored box. First, she unscrewed the compass from the top and handed it to the frizzy-haired, round-cheeked woman in the hooded robe, who worked it into a furrowed recess near the top of the bean at a slight slant. Then Magog unhooked the shiny panels from the sides of the box and handed them, one by one, to the amber-eyed women and the robed woman who, in consultation with Sam, positioned them amid the looping cables, where they attached magnetically.

From the stripped box, Magog withdrew a transparent, jelly-like orb, about the size of a softball; a set of crossed cutting blades suspended from an iron ring; and a misshapen blob of corroded metal and rock formed around the head of a hammer. These objects, too, were handed off for careful attachment to the silver bean.

The footlocker he'd retrieved from the basement of the antique store yielded a crab-shaped carving formed from blue lava rock; a tubular structure resembling a telescope; and a fistful of gold-leafed metal hooks. Several women went to work, twisting, connecting, inserting into slots these assorted items.

Magog now took the hand of a young girl, freckled with a divot in one cheek and her hair done up in auburn ringlets. With her free hand, the little girl clutched a crude straw-stuffed doll.

Once the final hook was screwed into place, everyone took several steps back, clearing a wide berth for Sam to step into with her mitered hat, her oily robe, and the black lacquered box.

"Welcome to all of you who have traveled near and far to attend this ceremony," Sam said to the group. "As you know, tonight is the culmination of years of preparation. We have successfully gathered from the four corners of the Earth all the precise materials needed to build Zgajar's Apparatus, according to the precise instructions of Serbian prophet Zgajar Strangis, confidant and contemporary of the great inventor Nicholas Tesla, and archon eponymous of the Secret Chiefs of the Hermetic Order of the Golden Dawn. Directions for the construction of Zgajar's Apparatus came to us as part of a cache of sacred tracts rescued eight years ago from beneath the floorboards of a hotel room in Calcutta, India, where English occultist Aleister Crowley once stayed."

Members of the gathering nodded, as if they all understood this much.

"At the heart of Zgajar's Apparatus is a silver-based alloy made with cadmium, gold, palladium, platinum, mercury, and, of course, silver. This material forms around a core of silver sandwiched with copper and graphite. Construction of the core alone took several months and the combined efforts of metallurgists from Peru and Argentina, whose work was fastidiously overseen by Saga Eldritch and several alchemists of her choosing."

The bald woman with the ungainly fingernails smiled and nodded as the gathering broke out in tasteful applause.

"The alloy base was then fashioned to Zgajar's exacting dimensions, and the shell was modified to accept the various connectors and inserts. The cable, which was made by hand, features braided 24-carat gold wire with insulation derived from a rare rubber tree in the Brazilian rainforest. The tubes along the top were also handmade; in this case, by an electrical engineer who specializes in creating replacement parts for outdated power transformers. And the list goes on and on. I won't bore you with all the details, but suffice it to say, every part of Zgajar's Apparatus was created to precise specifications using, in many cases, rare materials tooled by skilled craftspeople. The parts arrived through various channels over the course of several years. All of you helped in searching out these materials. And you all deserve congratulations for your various contributions to this project."

Another polite round of applause broke out.

Trevor frowned. *It was a machine. But no line cord connected it to any outlet, so it must not require electricity to operate.*

"If all goes right," Sam continued, "you will witness a sight beyond anything many of you have ever witnessed before—and with this group, that's saying a lot." This was met with a scattering of applause and a few chuckles. "Although it's not necessary, before we activate the device, let us say a brief prayer to our guiding spirit, the Goddess Dagon, in the words we have used since ancient days."

They bowed their heads and chanted, "Queen of the trident, queen of the sea. We, your loathsome, we, your vile, call to you."

Sam, still holding the black box, touched a panel on the back of the bean, and the vacuum tubes across the top glowed a bright orange. The cubed glass rods and the crab-shaped carving began throbbing a dim vermilion light. A mechanized hum filled the air, rattling the stained glass window Trevor stared through. Sam stepped to the right front, reached for a dial, and slowly turned it. The grooved rolling pins began rapidly spinning, and the foil strips fluttered at the ends of their bent copper appendages.

She adjusted another dial, and the spun pink glass began to writhe. A grouping of crystalline rods began wavering, their rigidity transformed suddenly into a more supple material that curled and uncurled like octopus tendrils.

She twirled another dial and the whole structure began rocking on its jointed wooden legs—like a mammoth mechanical bull—except the movements were more fluid and controlled.

Increasingly, the appendages groped out at the naked air toward the assembled women. It appeared to Trevor's eye as if this amalgamation of inanimate components had somehow fused into a living being. He fought the urge to run from the sight, instead remaining frozen in fascination.

Sam turned yet another dial, and blue light flooded from every mirrored surface. This blue light filled the basement, sweeping out over all of the gathering, and brightly illuminating the jars of oily liquid and the bonelike masses that were lined up in front of the apparatus.

Next, Sam began twisting the edges of the black box as if it were some kind of runic puzzle. Her hands moved steadily as she deftly maneuvered the panels of the box, sliding them, causing the box to transform into, first, a square block, then other contours altogether. The cube became a rhombus, then kite-shaped, then it transformed into something diamond-like, tapering to two sharp points. Each time it assumed a new form, Trevor noted a slight seizing of the bean, as if some inner mechanism was clicking into place. Sam worked her puzzle into a ridged cone, then a sort of tube, a hexagon sphere, and finally into something of an asymmetrical icosahedron.

Then, dramatically, she stopped.

She studied the final shape briefly, laid it on the carpet between the bean and the jars, and withdrew to the right side of Zgajar's Apparatus.

As Trevor looked on in wide-eyed amazement, the liquid in the jars began to swirl and foam, jostling the bonelike masses up and down in its oily wake. The prodded bones took on an eerie sheen and slowly expanded to the limits of their glass containment.

"Step back, everyone, and cover your eyes," Sam cautioned the crowd.

No sooner had they done so than the first jar splintered into a thousand jangly shards. The explosion jolted some observers from their feet and caused the basement's recessed lighting to flicker. The bonelike substance the jar had contained now flopped around on the carpet like a landed fish in what remained of the fluid.

The second jar detonated.

Now two of the boney objects were flipping around frantically, working to stretch beyond the limits of their dimensions. The first one unfolded and doubled its size. The second one struggled to do the same.

A third jar exploded, then a fourth. The crowd cowered but, like Trevor, could not pry eyes from the spectacle. Rolling and foundering amid broken glass and oily residue, four beings—ranging in size, roughly, from a jumbo Idaho spud to a yeasty loaf of bread dough—now squirmed maniacally across the carpeting.

The fifth and sixth jars erupted almost simultaneously, knocking out the basement's lights for good and sapping all the power from the house. As the music suddenly vanished, the largest of the creatures again doubled in size, while the others convulsed in jerky motions to catch up.

As the beings grew and grew, a greenish mist emitted from the bonelike smoothness of their outer shells. They developed cracks, then crevices that sank deep and ran with welling crimson. The largest of the monsters flowered open and bubbled up growths from its bloody center that resembled noxious, creeping stamen.

As one, the women fell to their knees and bowed their foreheads to the carpeted floor. All except Sam, who looked on in her mitered hat and oily robe like some skulking Druid chieftain. She turned and looked directly at Trevor, smiled joylessly, and tilted her head. "*Join us,*" she mouthed.

The beings swelled and bounced, flicking off bloody flecks. Their frames shivered and contorted into bloated, humanoid forms. Prodigious, ophidian eyes popped to the surface of the creatures' now solidifying, cratered skin. The eyes, gyrating violently, took in the groveling crowd and glared at them in an expression of sovereignty. Then the creatures stood, three-legged, belching smoke from newly fashioned mouths in hideous roars.

Trevor witnessed this in a daze, suddenly finding himself several steps removed from reality. All semblance of certainty developed over seventeen years of existence shook loose. His head spun. His gut became a whirlpool of freakish sensations.

Once again, Sam mouthed to him, "*Join us.*"

The next thing Trevor knew, he was running.

He bolted from the window and darted like a basketball center breaking for the net. Down the tree-lined road, rubber-soled sneakers slapping on the asphalt, panic shooting from his temples to his toes. He rounded the corner, visions of Zgajar's Apparatus, the frantic bone creatures, and the weird women still stirring his thoughts. Half-unaware of his surroundings, Trevor dodged through side streets, putting as much distance as possible between himself and the sandstone manor on Aldinach Trail.

Suddenly, headlights were in his face. The red and blue lights of a squad car came to life, the driver door swung open, and out stepped one of New Hope's finest.

"Are you alright, son? Is someone threatening you?"

Trevor gulped air and swiped sweat from his mouth. "The women ... I mean, what's going on in that house ... something unreal."

"Calm down, son," the cop said, gesturing with his hand. "What women?"

"I don't know. Witches, I guess."

"Witches?"

"Yeah. Or something. They have this machine. Zgajar's Apparatus they called it. It's kind of like a big silver bean, and it has all these wires and things attached to it."

"Silver bean?" The cop squinted at him, unsure what to make of this story. "Son, you haven't been popping pills or anything? Maybe smoking a little wacky weed with these women?" Then, after a pause, "Why don't we drive down to the station, and you can tell me all about the silver beans and the witch women?"

This was not what Trevor was hoping to hear.

"Let's just drive over to the house and take a look. You'll see. There's blue lights and ... alien creatures ... I still don't know what they were."

"And where is this house?"

"Aldinach Trail."

"Aldinach Trail? Hmm. That's a new one on me. Maybe we better go back to the station and round up some backup. You can never be too careful when it comes to dealing with witch women and alien creatures and such."

Back at the cop shop, Trevor told his story in a conference room to a trio of officers who fought hard to keep straight faces. A phone call was placed and Trevor's mom showed up, looking mortified.

He repeated the story for Mrs. Bates, whose jaw hung open the whole time.

Upon hearing the tale through to the end, Mrs. Bates asked the officers, "Is he in some kind of trouble?"

The older of the three waved at the air. "I can't see charging him with anything. Maybe he's had some kind of mental breakdown. I'm no psychologist."

"Why don't you just drive over to the house and see for yourselves," Trevor pleaded.

The older cop scratched his buzz-cut hair. "Tell you what, Trevor. You say this house full of witches is on ... what was it?"

"Aldinach Trail."

"On that wall right there is a map of New Hope." He pointed with a stubby finger. "You find Aldinach Trail on that map, and I will personally go there and interview the witch women. If it's not on the map, you go home with your mom, and you two can figure out the best course of action. Is it a deal?"

Of course, there was no Aldinach Trail on the map for Trevor to find.

On the car ride back, Trevor remembered the hundred dollars Sam had paid him. He fished the bills from his pocket and held them out for his mom to see. She glanced at them worriedly but said nothing.

In coming days, Trevor tried again and again to get someone to believe him: his sister, his father, his friends on the basketball team. But, not only were they all highly skeptical of his story, they were often downright rude to him. Even his own father told him to "quit talking like a nut job" and called him "a freak." His popularity at school began to tank. He became "that weird kid" that nobody wanted to mingle with. When he walked down the hall, classmates whispered and snickered.

No one believed him, and the more he spoke about it, the meaner their comments became. His talk about the whole adventure turned half-hearted and began to taper off. It got so Trevor began to wonder if maybe he wasn't off his rocker.

One day, he was walking around the area where he was convinced Aldinach Trail should've been, when another memory occurred to him. Gold letters over a doorway that read: "Those who speak of things that do not concern them shall hear things that will not please them."

Trevor walked home, and never mentioned his adventure to anyone ever again.

# SHADOW MAN

"Yesterday, upon the stair,
I met a man who wasn't there
He wasn't there again today
I wish, I wish he'd go away..."
—Hughes Mearns, "Antigonish"

A t one a.m. sharp, the figure in the fedora hat and cape appeared as he always did at that time on the sidewalk across Winnetka Avenue. Stooped and moving at a crawl beneath the streetlights, flies buzzing around his head, patches of moisture seeping through the gray flannel of his suit, he paused every few steps, making sure she got a good look at him, though the brim of his hat hid most of his face in shadow.

From her living room window, Jolaine Bronski watched this figure with pronounced wistfulness, rocking slowly and holding tight to the wooden box in her lap. Darkly grained, the box was proportioned large enough to accommodate a standard-sized baseball bat. Hieroglyphs were scrawled end to end across the surface, and to ensure Jolaine would not forget the meaning of the images, her mother had translated it for her often.

"After you say the words, rub the side of the box," Mother had instructed. "And remember, whatever you do, *do not open the box.* Promise me you will never open the box."

"I promise," she'd said, putting every fiber of assurance into the pledge.

Jolaine was not the sort of neighbor invited to coffee klatches. At best, her reputation was that of a misanthropic hermit; at worst, something much darker, something having to do with the occult and hexes and visiting bad juju on people who displeased her. The consensus by the Winnetka Avenue community was that, either way, it was best to stay off her radar altogether.

Rumors fueled these apprehensions.

Some years ago, for instance, the eldest son of the Kilgores next door had supposedly been rushed while taking out the garbage and accidentally spilled some candy wrappers on the ground that breezes blew onto Jolaine's front lawn. The boy failed to retrieve them. There the wrappers remained for several days. Then one morning the wrappers allegedly appeared on the front stoop of the Kilgores' home, along with a decapitated rooster.

As the figure in the fedora trod on, he slowly came undone. His outline wavered, expanded into airy bits, then disappeared in a waft of smoke. Jolaine wondered if anyone else ever saw him.

Sometimes, if the light was just right and the viewing angle aligned properly, unintended onlookers could catch glimpses from beyond. Usually, these peeks into the alternate universe came and went so quickly that a spectator passed them off as a hallucination. On rare occasions, though, these glimpses would last several minutes, leaving poor witnesses questioning their sanity.

Jolaine hadn't always been a recluse. In her younger days, she'd rebelled against restraint, prizing her liberty of movement above all else. She and Tanya Baker (and occasionally one of their lesser friends) spent their teenage evenings sneaking into St. Paul and Minneapolis nightclubs, brandishing fake IDs and sipping cocktails with strangers who asked them to dance. Sometimes, they crashed after-hours parties where the lights were turned off, the stereo turned up, and the flavorful smell of herb so thick, they could catch a buzz from just breathing the air.

Her mother and her father came from Chicago originally. They were spiritualists back in the day when spiritualism was widespread and embraced by many as a reasonable religious alternative. Mother, who favored yellow turbans and garments of purple linen, always carried herself with quiet dignity and grace. The second to fourth fingers of Mother's right hand were fused together, and under one soulful eye, she wore a star-shaped birthmark.

Father, always bolt upright and spotlessly clean, could've been a transplant from the nineteenth century with his formal manner, sharp creases, and walrus mustache. On rare occasions, he would give in to spurts of jocularity that caused his Adam's apple to bob in his throat.

Satisfied the specter was no longer roaming the sidewalks of New Hope, Minnesota, Jolaine rose from her rocking chair and returned the box to its secret place in the false bottom of the cabinet under the kitchen sink.

The table in the kitchen was the same oval of walnut she, her parents, and a parade of half-remembered strangers (and, occasionally, a few spiritualist family friends) had gathered around to contact the dead so many times so many years ago. Mother and Father, taking on mysterious personas, would sit at either end of the table facing one another, while the visitors would perch nervously at the long sides.

"From the wide, ancient skies of Baala Sheem," Mother's voice would boom, "where storm gods unsheathe swords of lightning, I call upon Valafar, succubus supreme in the nightmare army of Thamuz, queen of falsehoods."

She'd rub the box's side, delicately running her fingers over the hieroglyphic carvings.

"Valafar, who causes all shadows to fall, come from your coven of three, from the deep roots of your shoreless void to the side of your True Believer. I bid you, come to me."

Then she'd throw back her head, and all gathered at the table would clasp hands.

Jolaine always sat with her back toward the wall, next to Mother, clutching in her left palm one of the few dry and calm hands guaranteed to be in the room—the hand with the fused fingers. Jolaine's right hand never knew what it would get.

She remembered the smell of sweat, the dramatic, atmospheric tilt to unease or sometimes even distress when the lights went out; the squirming, the quick breaths, the moistening of lips.

Jolaine often wondered whether the wood of the box hidden below her sink came from an ironwood tree in the ancient desert of Baala Sheem. She liked to think it did.

Closing the doors beneath the sink, she returned to her living room window, where just this morning she'd watched a gaggle of Girl Scouts wheel a red wagon full of cookie boxes down the Kilgores' driveway to the sidewalk. They'd talked excitedly, having, no doubt, unloaded a bounty of Thin Mints or Peanut Butter Tagalongs at Jolaine's neighbors' house. She wouldn't have minded having a package or two of those tasty cookies herself, but she knew these Girl Scouts would never knock on *her* door. They wouldn't dare.

Sure enough, they'd walked past her house as if it was invisible, as if it wasn't even *there*, not even risking a surreptitious glance at it. That was the level of fear in which they held her.

When Jolaine was seventeen, Father passed to the Netherworld, and she took his place at the séance table. Mother had never discussed this new role with her. By all parties, it was just assumed she'd step in. At first, they practiced by having Valafar recall Father, who came whenever they beckoned, something not all spirits were eager to do. It was always good to hear from him, even if his disembodied voice came from a great distance, guided by Valafar through the ether to the dark surroundings of the kitchen. Sometimes, Jolaine could feel her father's presence, if not his touch.

She learned to adopt the mysterious pose, and donned linen and turban just like Mother so returnees could rest reassured that Father's demise hadn't severed their connection to the Netherworld. Dutifully, she held their moist hands as Mother bridged the great divide.

Afterward, when the visitors were gone and the box was again nestled in its secret place beneath the sink, it was *her* time. She'd change her clothes and vanish into the night, sometimes meeting up with a friend or two, sometimes bar-hopping by herself. Lonely young men complimented her, bought her drinks, and danced with her. From the gray confines of her spirit-welcoming house to the gaiety of the city after dark with its colored lights and sparkling disco balls, Jolaine transitioned effortlessly.

None of her encounters ever amounted to anything serious. The inevitable brush-off, polite but firm, always came at some point during the evening, usually early on but occasionally at closing time. The best-case scenario had Jolaine and her would-be Romeo parting after a wanking in the parking lot. Sometimes, phone numbers were exchanged, though she only gave false ones.

As old-fashioned as it may seem, her hesitancy to commit sexually stemmed from a belief that her maidenhead gave her a special power in both this world and the next, and it was a power she refused to relinquish to any man.

Year after year, Jolaine and her mother (with Valafar's assistance) continued to breach the eternal abyss for paying customers. So pervasive was the fame of the Bronski women in certain circles that clients came to them from as far away as Spain and Luxembourg.

MOTHER'S EVENTUAL DEATH came years later, many years after Father's, upending the workings of the family enterprise. Jolaine quickly found she had little enthusiasm for calling to Valafar and the spirit world for others' benefit. It wasn't that she was incapable of the feat, just that it didn't *feel* right anymore. Not sans the presence of Mother's grace and dignity, nor Father's ever-proper bearing. Not with outsiders in attendance.

Still, she tried anyway.

She approached some spiritualist friends of the family about joining her at the table, but competent as they were (to varying degrees), it wasn't the same. She even tried to teach her friend Tanya to play her second at the séances, to have a true pal's face looking back at her, but this attempt turned into a fiasco given Tanya's inexperience with the supernatural. Once, during the divination, she'd even heard Tanya struggle to maintain her composure.

Eventually, she gave up hosting public séances. Her parents had left her far from penniless, after all, and her years of performing under the yoke of the dollar seemed to Jolaine adequate, if less than fully satisfying.

71

This freed up her daytimes for wandering and nightly carousing.

She now had the limitless freedom she'd once craved. But in having it, she found it increasingly devoid of substance. Almost meaningless. Every day became more or less the same as every other. When she went out afternoons to a museum, concert, or play, she quickly became bored and disconnected from her environment. And, as the passage of time turned hopeful suitors ever-longer in the tooth, the city lights no longer shone as brightly and going out became more of a chore than an escape to merriment. Her nighttime excursions lessened to the point where she only went out once or twice a month. Often less.

Aside from the odd lunches and phone conversations with Tanya, nothing held immediacy for her anymore.

She increasingly spent her daytime hours daydreaming, watching television, sleeping, and slowly drifting into the morbidity that often plagues the solitary.

Approaching her late forties, virginity still intact, she became ever-drawn to the villainous side of magic. After all, thanks to the contents of the hieroglyphed box, the powers of deviltry remained at her beck and call.

Valafar put her in contact with the gone, and by studying her grimoires and practicing the duskier edges of the esoteric, she soon learned to materialize the spirits, sometimes even unleashing them on an unsuspecting world.

For instance, a cashier at Harbo's Garden Center who'd rolled his eyes at her when she asked him a question about chrysanthemums found at the end of a workday his car mysteriously filled with organic fertilizer. A Jehovah's Witness who knocked at her door one evening (despite the clearly worded NO SOLICITORS sign) kept finding, with each subsequent knock on other people's doors, the laces of his shoes tied together. One of her spiritual pranks was even famously reported in the media: the time she had the Christmas tree in front of the governor's mansion toilet-papered in protest of Republican Tim Pawlenty's 2002 election. And, of course, there was the candy wrapper incident with the Kilgores.

One day, she ran into her cousin Fatima at Half-Price Books in St. Paul. Fatima, who told fortunes and read the tarot at her home on University Avenue, suggested Jolaine join a Twin Cities coven.

*Yes. Of course.* Find others like herself and join them in their pursuits. Jolaine contacted family spiritualist friends, asked around, and, at last, located a gathering in Bloomington that wasn't Wiccan but of older roots. They welcomed her at once, and though their brand of esoteric led her yet further down the grim edge of magic, at least they brought new purpose to her mundane existence.

Then, just as she felt terra firma forming beneath her feet again, fate intervened unexpectedly, as fate often does. This time, it came in the form of Denny Loomis.

Glancing up from her tap beer at Wilebski's Blues Saloon in St. Paul, she locked on him instantly, on his Kelly-green eyes, on his camera-ready face and boyish lips as he asked her to dance. He was older than her by at least a decade, but the figure he cut in his fedora hat, gray-flannel suit, and whimsical black velvet cape was that of a younger, more virile man—one who still possessed the lightning character of the charismatic.

Jolaine, not one given to saccharine emotion or the doe-eyed enchantment known to be brought on by feminine observation of masculine eye candy, felt an overpowering swell of passion. As he led her to the dancefloor to the strains of G.B. Leighton's "I Got You," she realized, to her astonishment, that she'd just fallen in love.

OF COURSE, JOLAINE KNEW the sensation that afflicted her was just feel-good chemicals released by her brain. But, somehow, this knowledge took a back seat as her mind became preoccupied with the euphoria educed by memories of the dashing Denny Loomis.

"I don't know how this guy got his hook into me, Tanya," she'd confessed to her best friend over the phone. "But one look and he was reeling me in like a Lake Minnetonka walleye."

"Then what happened?"

She fingered the neckline of her blouse. "Well, we danced and we talked. He did most of the talking. I was sort of thrown off-balance by the whole experience. When I tried to speak, I just felt all balled up inside, and I'm afraid the few sentences that escaped my lips were featherbrained. He must think I'm a buffoon."

Tanya chuckled. "What did he tell you about himself?"

"Not much, really. He mostly commented on books, music, and movies. Not sure of his politics or religion. He did reveal that his first car was a Ford Mustang convertible. And he's apparently traveled quite a bit. He mentioned Mexico and the Bahamas."

"Did you give him your real phone number?"

She cringed. "I did. A complete stranger."

"That's a first."

"You don't suppose he's related to Ted Bundy, do you?"

"Let's hope not."

They both laughed this time, though in a reserved way.

"And this was Tuesday night, you say?" Tanya asked.

"Yeah. I know, it's been two days. Do you think he'll call?"

"Hard to say."

"I'm on pins and needles, Tanya."

"That's the thing about infatuation. It may feel good, but ultimately, you're its prisoner. But don't worry. If he doesn't call, you'll soon forget all about him. Unrequited desire fades eventually. It always does."

"Maybe." She was unconvinced.

That evening, he did call. From a club called The Night Before in northeast Minneapolis. They made a date for Saturday night. He could pick her up if she'd like.

The golden rule for a first date is that a woman NEVER gives out her home address. In case things go south. Jolaine knew this, but she told him where she lived anyway.

Did she even *know* herself anymore?

ON SATURDAY NIGHT, Denny Loomis arrived at her doorstep with a colorful spray of daisies, gardenias, and peonies. Once again impeccably dressed in gray flannel, fedora, and ever-present cape with its black lining and gold-colored collar buttons, Denny presented himself as the perfect gentleman, waiting patiently on the step as Jolaine hunted up a suitable vase for the flowers. She thought about inviting him in, but decided against it. She didn't want to risk her living room (with its pervasive skull motif) spoiling the mood.

They had a pleasant dinner at Cossetta's Italian Market on West Seventh Street in St. Paul. It was a beautiful evening, and after eating, they walked the city lanes, at one point holding hands, at another sharing a furtive kiss.

Like before, Denny did most of the talking, his smooth and confident patter putting her at ease, his slender hands gesturing exotically. She introduced a phrase of her own here and there, just to let him know she was still breathing, but she much preferred being carried off by the spell he wove with his reassuring words. As a result, she asked few questions and learned little new about him, other than that his favorite book was called *Dark House of Dreams*, the road he grew up on was Adeline Lane in Wayzata, and his mother's maiden name was Keller.

The next day, he called her, and they talked for hours on the phone. She learned he had a boyhood pet gerbil named Sorokin, that his first job was at Pearson's Candy Company in St. Paul, and other tidbits, such as where he was born (Shoreview), where he went to high school (Wayzata High School in Plymouth), and his favorite food (Pizza Margherita). Still, despite learning these details, he somehow remained a man of mystery: a shadow man.

After the call ended, Jolaine immediately dialed up Tanya.

"Did you learn anything more about him?"

"Yes and no. I know more details of his life, but I still don't feel I really know him as a person. You know what I mean?"

"Well, what do you talk about?"

She told Tanya what they'd discussed.

"I've dated men I knew a hell of a lot less about."

"You're a trusting soul, Tanya."

"And you're an intuitive one. Rely on your feelings."

"That's just it: I've never felt this way about anyone. I can usually read people quite accurately, but with him, my feelings are interfering with my sensors. All I get from him is white noise."

"And your oblong box doesn't help?"

"It probably could, but I'm afraid to use it that way."

"Afraid you'll learn something about him you don't want to know?"

75

"Everyone has secrets best left concealed. Awful things that we've moved beyond and become better people as a result of. I've found it best to leave these things about other people in the past. Knowing their darkest secrets needlessly colors my opinion of them."

This brought a thoughtful pause to their conversation. Then, Tanya asked, "Has he asked you for a second date?"

"Yes. Monday afternoon to Mickey's Diner. He's picking me up around noon. Then maybe go to a movie on Grand Avenue."

"Jolaine," she said cautiously, "does he know about your beliefs, Valafar and all that business?"

She gasped. "No, I never told him any of that. I thought I'd ease it into a discussion at some point. But I'm not trying to chase him off. I'll tell him, when I think the time is right."

"Then all I can say is enjoy your date and remember: keep things light. You don't have to *marry* the guy."


MICKEY'S DINER IN DOWNTOWN ST. PAUL is an eatery modeled after an old-fashioned railroad dining car. Dating back to 1937, the place is a bona fide landmark, a sort of crusty art deco-inspired joint known among locals for its reasonably priced rib-sticking food.

Jolaine and Denny sat elbow-to-elbow at Mickey's long, silver lunch counter, drinking coffee and eating buttermilk pancakes. They talked about the weather (cloudy, low-seventies), the food (chewy, nice texture), the people walking outside on the street, and other neutral topics where opinion didn't matter much.

After Denny ordered a refill on their coffee, Jolaine summoned up the courage to ask him about his cape.

He shrugged. "It's called a wanderer's cape. I bought it in Mexico. Not sure where it was made. It has arm holes, but I prefer wearing it off the shoulders. I know it's out of date by at least a hundred years, but I love how it feels on my back, and I get a lot of compliments on it. I guess it's sort of goth."

He grinned.

After lunch, having decided nothing was worth watching at the local cinemas, they drove to Como Park, toured the glass-cased conservatory with its lovely plants and flowers, and frittered away the afternoon. They were crossing the Como Park footbridge when her phone rang.

It was Tanya. "Listen, Jolaine. I thought of something a bit unsettling. About your shadow man. Something you told me about him didn't sit right with me. I finally figured out what it was."

Jolaine glanced at Denny, who stood at the pinnacle of the stone railing, looking onto the path below. She turned her back on him and stepped away. "Go on."

"Well, maybe it's just a coincidence, but when I was signing onto an old investment account, I forgot my password. So, I had to reset it. Before I could, I had to answer some security questions."

"Okay."

"Well, the questions were things like, what's my mother's maiden name? What's the name of a childhood pet? Where was I born? Where did I go to high school? The same topics you said Denny brought up. When he gave you his answers, I suppose you gave him yours?"

Jolaine felt a chill in her blood. "Yes." She again glanced at Denny's back. "I did."

"Just be careful. I'm not saying he was, but he could have been fishing for information to gain access to your banking or credit card accounts."

"Thanks, Tanya. I'll keep it in mind."

She hung up and eyed him as he turned to face her.

Was her caped companion just a dapper conman?

HE DROPPED HER OFF AT HER HOUSE in the late afternoon. His goodbye kiss was passionate, and she knew he wanted her to invite him inside, but she resisted.

Standing at her front window, she watched Denny Loomis pull away into the traffic of Winnetka Avenue, wishing she'd never met him, never succumbed to his charismatic charm, never felt love's gossamer caress nor the dread that behind this feathery touch could lurk a sledgehammer targeting her heart.

Stepping to the kitchen, she retrieved the box and laid it on the oval séance table.

It was Grandfather John, her father's father, who'd first discovered the container back in 1921. The way Mother had told the story, Grandfather was working as a cataloguer of artifacts at the Field Museum in Chicago.

"Relocating the huge collection was an enormous undertaking," Mother had said. This was right after the museum opened at its current location at Grant Park on Lake Shore Drive. The original building was in Jackson Park at the former Palace of Fine Arts, which now houses the Museum of Science and Industry. Money for the new structure came from department-store magnate Marshall Field, who left it to the city in his will. "Workers moved the artifacts over in crates on rails and in horse-drawn carriages. Grandfather, a devotee of Aleister Crowley and the Hermetic Order of the Golden Dawn, was conducting a final run-through of the Jackson Park building when a step in the stairs to the basement gave him an odd sensation."

Here, Mother's eyes had noticeably widened. "Inspecting the step, he discovered the tread board was hinged. When he opened it, he found inside a secret compartment containing that box wrapped in black cloth. When he touched it, he knew at once that he'd just come into possession of a magical relic. Instead of transporting the box to the new museum location, he brought it home, where he studied its history and the meaning of its hieroglyphs."

He determined the writing on the box was nearly two thousand years old and was a product of the Indus Valley in the Indian subcontinent. The Indus people were one of the three earliest civilizations known to humanity. Though it took him several months to translate the writing, he never opened the box out of respect for its magical properties and concern over what it might unleash. And, sure enough, as he deciphered the ancient writing, he read that opening the box would cause instant death to the person who opened it.

"There's nothing about the box or its contents in formal archeology books," Mother had said, "but your grandfather found a mention of it in the writings of Russian spiritualist Helena Blavatsky. As far as she knew, a Hindi mystic named Rishi Mahindra last owned the container, and it was handed down to him from a Kshatriya sorcerer whose ancestor once battled with the demon Valafar while passing through the

Mideastern desert land of Baala Sheem. During the battle, he sliced off the demon's arm and drove the fiend off with a Kshatriya spell. The ancestor kept the arm as a mystic souvenir of his bravery and locked it up in this box, sealing it with a hex. He then brought it back to his warrior family in the Indus Valley.

"The family soon discovered that the arm, having once been attached to Valafar, could still serve as a conduit to the demon through which, by using certain incantations, they could contact and communicate with the fiend.

"They quickly learned that the demon was desperate to reclaim its arm," Mother continued. "According to the brute, although the arm was cleanly severed in this world, it remained attached in other planes of existence, forming ethereal links that could be exploited by one of Valafar's many otherworldly enemies to launch a blindside attack and possibly destroy the demon. The succubus supreme in the nightmare army of Thamuz felt suddenly vulnerable.

"The family refused to give up the arm but made a pact with the fiend: they would guard the box with Kshatriya magic—even protect it from ever being opened—if Valafar would serve as their pipeline to the spirit world. Though a pact with a demon can never be fully trusted, Valafar honored this one, and the Indus sorcerers used the box with the severed arm as a bridge to the land of the dead, and, in their runic script, they wrote instructions on how to use it, including the chant for calling up the demon and an admonishment to always safeguard the box from ever being opened."

Here, she pointed a finger at Jolaine.

"The arm passed through generation after generation," Mother went on, "until it was discovered among other artifacts, on a Field Museum expedition to the African Congo, of all places. How it got there, how it eventually got hidden in a false stair in a former Chicago exhibition hall's basement, who knows? But fate or luck brought it to our family, and with it, the power to connect with the Netherworld."

Remembering this story now, Jolaine tipped the box one way, then the other, and felt its grim contents roll back and forth.

ULTIMATELY, SHE STUCK to her guns and didn't call on Valafar to open the conduit to the spirit world where she could ask about Denny. After all, when it came to suspecting his intentions, she had little more than a hunch, and hadn't he always treated her with gentlemanly kindness and respect?

After their third date, Jolaine reached deep into her fortitude to find the strength to welcome him beyond the threshold of her secret world. "Would you like to come in?"

Standing on her doorstep, Denny brightened. "Nothing would please me more," he said.

They'd spent the early evening touring the Minneapolis Sculpture Garden, a well-maintained, eleven-acre park featuring roughly sixty pieces of artwork, including the delightful *Spoonbridge and Cherry*, a fountain sculpture featuring a fifty-foot spoon holding a giant cherry, reminiscent of the pop-art movement of the 1960s. Afterward, he'd treated her to a Greek salad and avocado toast at Cardamom, the adjacent hillside eatery.

Now, he silently took in her living room, a chamber Tanya once described as "a perfect tribute to the Catacombs of Paris." Here, skull art dominated: a hundred or better representations of the human cranium—plain, jeweled, baroque, gold-gilded, abstract, futuristic, you name it. Some were elegant, some frighteningly crude, fashioned from raw clay, wood, ceramics, or metal. Paintings of skulls hung on the walls. Skull-decorated table lamps lit the room.

"You have quite a collection," he observed.

"My grandfather started collecting them. He passed them on to my parents, who added to the hoard. Some are quite old and, I imagine, quite valuable."

For an instant, she thought she saw his eyes sparkle.

"And this symbol?" he asked, nodding to the floor.

Carved into the red oak, a huge pentagram with runic characters leered up at them. "It's my religion, Denny. If you want me in your life, you must allow me my beliefs."

He cleared his throat. "Of course. It's just a lot to digest right off the bat."

*Well, maybe he wouldn't be scared off after all.*

She'd dodged questions about religion on their dates, but now that the subject had been broached, she came clean with him, or as clean as she could without divulging any family arcanum. They settled into chairs at the kitchen séance table and sipped spiced wine. She talked. He listened.

As she spoke about Valafar and the box, she felt as though she was seesawing between two worlds: Denny's world of the rational and hers of the celestial. It took an effort to retrieve the container and set it before him on the table.

"Can I touch it?"

"Yes. But don't open it. Opening it would be fatal."

"You're joking?" But he quickly saw she was not. "Not to challenge your beliefs, Jolaine, but it seems … far-fetched … that a demon's arm could be in this container. Haven't you ever been tempted to peek inside?"

"Never. I know what's inside. It's the right arm of Valafar, one of the famous Three Devils of Baala Sheem, and an ancient curse protects it."

"You honestly believe that, *physically*, the right arm of a demon is in here?"

"Yes. Physically."

He cupped his chin with one hand and drummed lightly on the oblong box with his other.

THAT NIGHT, they consummated their relationship, and, to her surprise, the Earth didn't shatter, the sky didn't fall, and afterward, she felt about the same as she had before.

Aside from some initial discomfort, it was not an altogether unpleasant experience. In fact, she found herself relishing the closeness. Denny was slow and gentle. He braced on his elbows to keep his weight from bearing down on her, and his kisses were abundant and intoxicating. Thankfully, she didn't bleed, as she feared she might.

Then they talked softly for a while, this new familiarity bonding her closer to him than ever before. *How could I ever have mistrusted him?*

She slipped off to a peaceful sleep—the calming dark ebbing and flowing over her.

At one a.m. sharp, she awoke to a noise from the kitchen: the muted squeal and thump of a cabinet door opening and closing.

She sat up. He wasn't in bed with her. *Probably getting a drink of water.*

She lay back down and started falling asleep again when a piercing scream and howl tore through her lethargy. Downstairs, a hand slapped wood, a chair overturned. She stood, grabbed a linen housedress from her chifforobe, and scrambled into the hallway and down the stairs, taking them two at a time. The howl turned quickly to sobs that fragmented into grotesque grunts and tortured wheezing.

"Denny!" she shrieked. "Are you alright?"

Breathing heavily, she made her way to the kitchen. The light was on, but there was no one there.

"Denny?"

She looked at the box on the table and her heart sank.

JOLAINE REPORTED HIM MISSING the next day. What else could she do? His car still sat in her driveway. A policeman, chewing a toothpick, took down information on a little notepad.

"Just disappeared in the middle of the night?" The cop's eyes narrowed as he studied her. "And you suspect foul play?"

"I woke up, and he was just gone. Does that seem normal?"

The cop took in her collection of decorative skulls without comment. His partner, a big woman straining the buttons of her uniform, walked back and forth from the kitchen to the living room, hands on her hips, saying nothing.

"And he told you his name was Loomis?"

She nodded. "Denny Loomis."

"Did he take anything of yours with him?"

"What do you mean?"

"Is anything missing? Any valuables?"

"Not that I've noticed. Why?"

"About a month ago, we received a warning to be on the lookout for a guy who matches your Denny's description. A conman out of Milwaukee who's wanted for questioning on charges of identity theft, auto theft, and various other crimes."

She felt a pang. "And that's Denny? Are you sure?"

The cop stopped writing on his pad. "We don't get many folks in New Hope who wear fedora hats and capes. And that car in your driveway was reported stolen from a parking lot in Eau Claire, Wisconsin. I'd say the odds are pretty good that your Denny is our fugitive."

That's when Jolaine Bronski swore off nightclubs for good, as well as plays, concerts, and restaurants, choosing instead to retreat into the bleakness of her tragedy-stricken life. She cut all ties with Tanya and seldom left her house except occasionally late at night to run an errand or meet up with her coven.

All day and night, she kept her drapes drawn to fend off inquisitive neighborhood busybodies, with one exception. Her living-room curtains parted each morning at one a.m. sharp, and she cast a wistful eye on the figure in the fedora hat and cape that appeared strolling on the sidewalk across the street.

Denny Loomis, with the brim of his hat shadowing his face, and a mist of flies buzzing all around him, and the moldy dankness of death leaking through his once-pristine flannel suit, always came for her. Always gave her a chance to join him.

From her window, Jolaine Bronski watched, slowly rocking in her chair, clutching to her lap the wooden container now stained with Denny's blood. The blood left on the box from the print of the hand that had slammed it shut after he'd opened it and the ancient curse had claimed him. The bloody handprint clearly showed the impression of Mother's three fused fingers.

"I saved you, Jolaine," Mother told her from beyond the veil. "He'd left the lid off. If you'd come downstairs with the box still open, you would have shared his fate."

But every morning, Jolaine wondered if she wouldn't prefer haunting the streets of New Hope hand-in-hand with her caped lover, conman or not. She rolled the arm back and forth within its oblong container, fingers resting on the cover, knowing she could always join him.

All it would take was a flick of her wrist.

# IT CAME OUT OF THE SKY

"Those who have never seen a living Martian can scarcely imagine the strange horror of its appearance."
—H.G. Wells, *The War of the Worlds*

N ow, do you believe me?" Jeb Greavor asked, his thin lips quivering in his bone-lean, beard-stubbled face.

Mace Stangis stared wide-mouthed at the smoking hole and the smoldering twist of metal within it. "Holy shit." A sparkle of dread tingled in Mace's stomach.

"What do you s'pose it is?" Jeb asked.

"I could ask you the same thing."

Jeb poked at the hole's contents with a booted foot. "It's a light metal. Aluminum maybe." He leaned in for a closer look. "Smells something awful."

It was early evening in the dead of August. Jeb had called up his neighbor and fishing buddy, Mace, and told him some kind of meteor had just crashed in Jeb's back forty acres.

"What?" Mace had asked, wondering if Jeb wasn't pulling his chain.

"I'm not kidding you, kid. Come over and see for yourself."

"You're asking me to leave my favorite chair, a cold beer, and a Twins game on TV? This better be good. They're beating the pants off the Yankees right now."

"I need you to come out. The damn thing's smoking like a steam engine out there, and I gotta try to keep it from setting Yancy's corn on fire." Bill Yancy was the farmer to whom Jeb had been leasing his acreage since retiring from farming five years ago.

The tone of Jeb's voice convinced Mace this wasn't a gag. He set down his beer, pulled on his jeans and his wide-brimmed straw hat, and climbed into the rust-bucket 1950 Chevy 3150 pickup he'd recently bought at an estate sale in nearby Sebeka, Minnesota. The engine was prone to missing and sputtering, it got just eight miles to the gallon, and the odometer was permanently frozen at 999,999, but he'd gotten the old crate for a steal and it ran well enough to get him to town and back.

Two miles and a quarter-gallon of gas later, Mace pulled into the gravel driveway and found Jeb in the front yard, gesticulating like a jug-eared puppet with a bucket of water and a handful of dripping towels. "C'mon, kid. Hurry."

It was funny that Jeb always called him "kid" when Mace was six months older than him. But, when you get to your golden years, age becomes relative.

He climbed out of the truck and chased Jeb around the corner of the weather-beaten farmhouse to the side yard. Sure enough, in the midst of the cornfield, white smoke billowed like it was coming from a fog machine.

They ran as fast as their seventy-year-old legs would carry them, thrashing down furrows of corn until they reached the source of all that smoke. Jeb emptied the water jug into a hole about four feet wide and steam hissed back at them. Mace used the wet towels to knock flames from a circle of cornstalks. When they were certain the risk of fire had abated, they inspected the hole.

Wedged in it, a hollow chunk of metal capsule, flayed open on one side, beamed up at them from a veil of rising haze. The early-evening light penetrated deep enough into the exposed casing for them to make out some kind of circuitry.

"Maybe some kind of drone gizmo?" Jeb ventured after he'd poked it with his foot, and they'd asked one another what they thought it was in that hole.

"I don't know. Looks pretty elaborate for a toy. Maybe some NASA machine?"

Jeb ran an arthritic hand across his balding scalp. "Shouldn't we report this to somebody?" he asked, still breathing heavy.

"I think so. Maybe we should just call 9-1-1." Mace took off his hat and rubbed a forearm across his sweating forehead. With his free hand, he was fishing in a pocket for his cell phone when Jeb stopped him.

"S'pose it's ... something else?"

"What do you mean, 'Something else?'"

"Something, I don't know, *alien*?"

Mace was about to tell his old friend he'd been watching too many shows on the Syfy Network, but staring down at that smoldering chunk of metal, he withheld the sarcasm. "Well, whatever it is, we should let bigger brains than ours figure it out."

"Maybe…" Jeb's craggy old face turned grim. "Maybe not."

"What do you mean?"

Jeb jutted out his jaw and a look of determination swept his features. "I've seen on the internet where people report things like this to the government and men in black show up, haul the object away, and threaten them not to tell anyone anything, *or else*."

"Men in black? Like the movie?"

"Something like that. But if you ignore their warnings, they'll blackball you and have everyone thinking you're a kook. Maybe send you to the loony bin."

That sounded farfetched to Mace, but he wasn't a hundred-percent certain of anything at the moment. "How do you suppose that casing got tore open like that?"

"Looks to me like something powerful wanted out."

Mace flopped his hat back on and pointed. "Well, looks like that something might've worn a path through the corn over there."

Jeb turned and looked. Sure enough, not far away, the maize cleaved open in a ragged trail.

"Should we follow it?" Mace asked.

"Let me get my shotgun first. Just in case."

*Well, it didn't hurt to be prepared for whatever.* "Hey, Jeb. Maybe get two."

SHOTGUNS AT THE READY, they entered the corn furrow and moved in single file, with Jeb in the lead. Night was gathering, and the stars were popping out in the darkening slate-blue sky. The moon, what Mace's dad had called the Barley Moon, cast a silver glow on the two old-timers, the surrounding corn, and the path ahead.

They tread cautiously, ears perked, shoulders hunched a bit.

"Jeb," Mace said, "you really think this is a good idea?"

"Don't go yellow on me, kid."

"But, I mean, let's get a few others to go with us, at least. Maybe Herb Menshaw and his boys—"

"Shhhh! Listen."

They went quiet.

"I don't hear nothing," Mace said after a minute.

"And you won't either if you keep running your mouth."

The path through the cornstalks cut at slight angles but ran more or less in a straight line. They walked the field for about fifteen minutes before Jeb piped up, "This runs right to Bill Yancy's place. C'mon!"

They jogged, tearing through the stalks and the blades and the leaf sheaths with shotguns at port arms. The August heat opened all of Mace's pores, and the dread of a confrontation with who-knows-what worked at him until he felt numb and lightheaded. From ahead came the sounds of an animal screaming.

The two men crashed into a clearing and, shoulder to shoulder, came to a sudden stop.

"Holy mother of mercy," Mace said.

In the fenced-in grazing area in back of Yancy's farmhouse lay a shearling in a puddle of blood, stomach ripped open, trembling in the final agonies of death. Hunkered over the poor creature, a form three feet tall, shaped vaguely like a little man but possessing the characteristics of a savage beast, voraciously nourished itself on a mouthful of dangling intestines. Covered in gray reptilian skin with spikes running down its back, the monster gouged into the lamb, shredding through ribs and vertebrae and flaps of hide with razor claws, slinging blood high into the night sky. A drop of it flew all the way to Jeb and landed on his boot.

"Errrrggghh!" he moaned, stepping backward, trying to kick the blood drop from his toe.

At this noise, the monster's head snapped up and stilled, its eyes glowing malevolently at the two old-timers.

Jeb, who Mace always thought was one of the bravest men he knew, dropped his shotgun to the dirt and started shaking all over. His knees went loose and he swooned.

Mace grabbed him by the shirt collar and shouted at him. "Let's get out of here!"

Just then, Bill Yancy, towheaded and all of thirty-four, stumbled bowlegged from his house in his striped boxers, holding a bolt-action Springfield rifle that must've been older than Mace's beater pickup.

"Who goes there?" Yancy asked like some army sentry. Then his eyes widened to the size of silver dollars and his mouth flopped open. "What the—"

The beast glared at Yancy, glared at the old-timers, and, with a clawful of sheep gore and intestines still hanging from its mouth, sprang a good ten feet into the air. The Springfield barked. Mace, having no luck budging Jeb, swung his long-barrel and fired a volley of pellets. He wasn't sure who hit it, him or Yancy, but he saw the monster flinch midair. It hit the ground jumped again, higher than before, and, next thing he knew, it was off into the night.

Jeb fainted.

Yancy ran to his shearling, which was fully dead by then, and stood looking at the poor thing for a minute. Then he hurried over and Mace met him at the fence.

"What the hell was that?" Yancy said, looking oddly dignified in his boxer shorts.

Mace shrugged. "Whatever it was, it looks like it landed in some kind of missile. Jeb saw it come down in his back forty and he called me."

"Jeb? Where is he?"

Mace turned and pointed. "Back there. Must be in shock or something."

Yancy exited through a gate, and together they walked over to where Jeb was coming to, sitting up, woozy.

"You alright?" Mace asked.

"I'm fine, kid," Jeb said. "Don't know what came over me."

They helped him to his feet.

"Let's show this UFO of ours to Yancy, and hear what he thinks about it," Mace said.

They trudged back through the cornfield, Mace leading the way this time, Jeb next, moving wobbly, and then Yancy, still wearing only his striped boxers. They came to the hole where the object had landed, only now the capsule or missile or whatever it was had reduced itself to a bubbling pool of what looked like mercury.

They watched it fizz and burble and slowly sink into the ground until all trace of it was gone.

"We should tell someone about this," Mace said, breaking a long silence.

"Tell who?" Jeb said. "Tell 'em what? That an alien rocketship landed in my backyard, but it's not there anymore? That a visitor from outer space popped out of it, ran through the cornfield, gutted one of Yancy's sheep, then bounced off into the night? *You* want to tell *that* to somebody?"

Jeb had a point. Who'd believe them when they could hardly believe it themselves?

NONE OF THEM SLEPT THAT NIGHT. Instead, they gathered around Jeb's kitchen table (Yancy still in his boxers), drinking Grain Belt beers, telling and retelling their evening's adventure and debating strategy.

"Did you ever see such a thing?" Yancy asked, not expecting a response after the seventh time he posed the question.

They pooled their observations, examined them from every angle, and kept coming to the same conclusion: a dangerous creature from outer space might be running amuck in the countryside, but they couldn't tell anyone about it without sparking rumors on the faltering nature of their sanity.

"Listen," Jeb said. "One of us shot the thing, right?"

Two heads bobbed.

"So, for all we know, the creature might already be dead."

Mace and Yancy agreed.

"So, let's not get ahead of ourselves. Give it a day or two, and if nothing else happens, we're home free. Had us a nice little adventure. No one has to know about it."

Yancy rubbed his hands on his bare knees and began to fidget. "But what if it isn't dead? What if it's still out there somewhere, killing livestock or God knows what?"

"People," Mace said. "What if it's out there killing people?"

They took on grave expressions.

Then Jeb said, "It didn't kill us, did it? Didn't even try."

"Maybe we got lucky," Yancy said.

But, when the first light of day peeked into the kitchen window, no one had come up with a better plan. Sit and wait, keep their ears and eyes open, and hope for the best.

Mace hoped no poor soul ended up paying for their silence.

Yancy slapped his meat hooks on the table. "Well, I got to go. I'm not like you boys, retired and all. I still got a farm to run. Bella's in Bemidji visiting her sister Charlotte, but she'll be back today and I'll have to tell her something. She'll notice the lamb's gone. Guess I could say a wolf got hold of it." He eyed the two old-timers but appeared to be looking through them. "I've been married to that woman fifteen years, and I've never once lied to her. Guess there's a first time for everything."

And he was out the door.

A DAY PASSED. Then two. No movement in the cornfield; no reports of livestock being mauled. Nothing out of the ordinary was seen or heard of. They began resting easier.

Mace was in the living room of his old farmhouse, doing a crossword puzzle in his favorite chair, when his cell phone rang. He fished it from the cushion beneath him and saw on the caller ID it was Jeb.

"What's an eight-letter word for excessively enthused?" Mace asked.

"A what?"

"An eight-letter word for excessively enthused. I'm doing a crossword puzzle."

"Forget about that. We got something more serious to attend to."

"Like what?"

"You know what. Now get your boney ass over here. I've gotta show you something."

The sky was overcast, not with rain clouds but with brown smoke from the massive wildfires blazing across western Canada. At last count, the fires had burned through roughly twenty-five million acres—an area about the size of Kentucky—polluting the skies and triggering air-quality alerts in hundreds of cities across the U.S. On bad days like this one, people with breathing difficulties, as well as youngsters and the aged, were advised to stay indoors. Scientists claimed the smoke from these fires was worse for your lungs than auto emissions. The smell and taste alone could be awful.

Wisps of the smoke made their way to ground level, wrapping Jeb's house in haze.

The front door popped open and Jeb, wearing a Christmas scarf over his mouth and carrying his two shotguns, hurried out as Mace's old pickup puttered up the driveway. Mace dug a leftover Covid mask from the truck's glove compartment and climbed out to meet him.

"This better be good," Mace said. "We shouldn't be walking around in this mess."

Jeb, looking like some bandit from a Western with the scarf over his face, handed Mace one of the shotguns. "Well, you're going to want to see this, kid."

They trudged across Jeb's back forty, to the location where they'd watched the UFO evaporate, and a bizarre sight met their eyes.

The edge of the hole left by the impact had sprouted a red, phosphorescent mold that followed along the fringes of the trail the creature had left in the cornfield.

Mace knelt for a closer inspection.

"Don't touch it," Jeb warned.

"Right." Mace retracted the finger that had been inches from the stuff. He was now doubly glad to be wearing the mask. Maybe he should've also worn gloves.

The mold, then about an inch wide, had a dense and nasty texture. Besides being a luminescent coppery red, furry white and green spots peppered its surface. It looked particularly eerie in the muted light let through by the Canadian smoke.

"What do you make of that?" Jeb asked.

Still kneeling, Mace shook his head. "I've never seen anything like it."

He rose, and they followed the trail, being careful to keep the fungus from getting on their boots. Once again, they made their way to Yancy's fenced-in back pasture. The mold traced a path, in and out, past Yancy's fence, leading to and from the bloodspot left by the mutilated lamb. Yancy and his wife, Bella, a fleshy, heavy-boned woman with stumpy arms and legs and a vaguely Italian-featured face, stood in the grazing area, looking pale and shaken.

Jeb and Mace, still masked, let themselves in through the gate.

Yancy looked up at them in disbelief. "What in the name of all that's holy causes something like *that*?"

Mace glanced at Bella and nodded, not sure how much he could say in front of her.

"It's alright," Yancy said. "I told her everything. Not sure she believed any of it until this happened."

"So, you boys are saying this alien thingy that killed our shearling and gallivanted through our cornfield left behind this red stuff?" Bella asked.

Mace shrugged.

Bella coughed.

"That thing we saw could've left behind spores or something on the ground," Jeb said.

"Hell, the way it jumped around, it wasn't even touching the ground most of the time," Yancy said. "But still it left a trail you could probably see glowing from outer space." He went a shade paler. "You don't suppose crop insurance covers alien mold, do you?"

Bella coughed again. Mace knew she had a touch of asthma and this smoky air wasn't doing her any good.

"Let's get you inside before you cough out a lung," Yancy said. "I'll grab one of those stupid Covid masks and go along with Jeb and Mace to see how extensively this mold damaged our corn."

Yancy was one of these Covid skeptics who feared the government was using the pandemic as an excuse to exercise its totalitarian, leftist control on its citizens, but he'd gone along with the mask-wearing and the inoculation jabs for Bella's sake when she argued that people with conditions like hers were especially vulnerable to the disease. One of Yancy's uncles and two of his cousins had refused the vaccinations which, Mace figured, explained why they now rested in perpetuity in Sebeka's Evergreen Cemetery.

Yancy reemerged from his farmhouse toting his ancient rifle and wearing a mask that Bella had sewn during the pandemic. She'd made it from leftover scraps of a blanket she'd fashioned for one of Yancy's nephews. It featured SpongeBob SquarePants, Patrick Star, and Squidward Tentacles looking goofy in front of an underwater pineapple.

"Don't say a word," Yancy warned. They didn't. No one was in a joking mood.

They traced the creature's tracks through the smoke, deep into the cornstalks, the edges of the path lit by the crimson glow. They came upon the ravaged remains of what might have been a fox. It was hard to tell. Farther down the path, they arrived at a cottontail rabbit in similar condition.

"Looks like our alien has been a busy boy," Jeb said softly.

They cautiously moved several yards farther down the trail, when an angry, scuffling sound shook them like a bolt from the blue. Ahead, just visible between the pillars of corn, the beast from the other night had a rodent cornered in an area of flattened stems and was shifting in for the kill.

Mace never thought he'd feel sorry for a vole, but he did now.

Crashing into the shallow clearing of crushed husks and broken shafts of maize, the three men raised their weapons chest-high.

Alerted, the monster wheeled toward them, and the vole scampered to safety. When the guns roared, the gray reptilian beast was already in the air, out of their line of fire and descending on them with razor claws flashing. Despite the obvious injury on one side from the previous night's shooting, the creature seemed more ornery than hurt when it landed atop Yancy's golden locks and began ripping into his skull.

Mace knocked the alien to the ground with the butt of his shotgun.

Yancy had blood cascading from his head wounds in a steady surge, down his neck and shoulder, and slopping to the soil. It seemed like he no longer knew where he was.

Jeb fired his shotgun and the alien may have caught a few pellets, but that was one speedy little devil; it rolled from the brunt of the blast to its feet and charged the shooter, baring drool-glistened fangs.

Mace smelled the feral, carrion stench on the creature's breath as it lunged, and he could see Jeb's knees giving out. Mace's shotgun roared again. This time, he caught the filthy alien in a broadside gut shot that had the beast rolling and flopping on the ground. It took a full three minutes for the thing to die, then Mace pumped another shot into it for good measure.

LATER, ON THAT AUGUST DAY, Mace watched Herb Menshaw and his boys in their Ram 2500 brake on the gravel road that ran between Jeb's place and Yancy's. The worst of the smoke had lifted and the twinkling lights of the police, the sheriff's department, and the ambulance danced across the truck's steel grille. A deputy made a hand signal for the Ram to turn around and go back the way it came. The deputy and Herb jawed amiably a bit, then the pickup executed a three-point turnabout and was gone.

A helicopter landed in the dust and gravel of the road, and emergency-medical technicians scrambled to get the unconscious Yancy onboard in a stretcher. The ground EMTs, who'd been first on the scene in their wailing truck ambulance, had wrapped his head in bandages, but he'd already lost a lot of blood. Bella, still wearing one of her SpongeBob masks, lugging an oversized purse, climbed in dutifully behind Yancy and an air EMT, and, in a shot, the chopper whirled off into the smoky sky, headed for the Mayo Clinic in Rochester, over 250 miles away.

The ground EMTs tried to lead Jeb into their hospital wagon, but he adamantly refused. He said there was nothing wrong with him but a few scratches and scrapes he'd suffered as a result of fainting in the corn.

They applied some Band-Aids and made him sign a piece of paper refusing transport, then drove away. Jeb might've thought he was okay, but Mace wasn't completely sold. Something about him didn't look right.

Mace had already been cleared by the EMTs to stay behind and answer questions from the police and the sheriff's deputies, and later from the FBI people and the government cleanup crew, so that's what Jeb and Mace did. They told them everything, exactly as they remembered it, though Mace did most of the talking.

The local cops were incredulous, as you'd expect them to be, but the feds didn't even blink. It was like a monster dropping out of the sky was a routine matter.

The cleanup folks wore protective suits as they hauled out a vanful of evidence, including the alien corpse, everything bundled in white plastic sacks. Once they had what they needed, they went back out in the cornfield and did a controlled burn of the whole forty acres. Then they got in their vehicles and also left.

By the time the Twin Cities news media showed up, it was nearing dark, and the field was already reduced to scorched stubble.

No men in black ever showed, and the FBI people never told Mace or the others not to say anything about their alien experience, but the story the feds gave the press was that a strain of *E. coli* pathogen had been identified in the field and the acreage was destroyed purely as a precaution.

Before the last FBI agent left, Mace asked her whether the government expected them to stick to the official story.

"Say whatever you want," she answered. "It's a free country. Maybe someone will believe you." She didn't seem to care much about it either way.

She gave him one of her cards, got into a black sedan, and drove off, leaving Mace and Jeb alone in an eerie quiet.

INCLUDING REST AND SNACK STOPS, it took them almost five hours to get to Mayo Clinic Hospital in Rochester. They pulled up in Jeb's 2020 Ford F-150 in the Graham Parking Ramp across the street from the hospital at about three-thirty in the morning.

After stopping at the information desk, they located Bella in a family waiting room, pacing and grinding her teeth. She resembled the walking dead.

"What are the doctors saying?" Mace asked.

She stopped pacing and began wringing her stumpy fingers. "Bill's hurt pretty bad. That space monster really did a job on him, I guess."

Mace reached out to comfort her, but she backed away. "What do you mean, 'Did a job on him?'"

"I mean, got its claws into him pretty deep, cracked his skull, and might've done some brain damage. They're still running tests, trying to figure out what all's wrong with him, but it's not looking good."

Jeb, looking more haggard than Bella, trudged to a chair and flopped down, scratching at a bandaged elbow.

"How are you, Jeb?" Bella asked.

He waved away her concern. "Just a couple of scratches. The medical guys said I should get some rest. How are you holding up?"

"Don't know which end is up anymore. They have him in isolation, so I can't visit him right now. These people are nice enough, but they haven't brought me any news for a while. You sure you're alright?"

"Sure."

"When Jeb passed out, he went down like a jig sink," Mace said. He leaned toward his friend. "Haven't seen you that out of it since that night at the cabin when you got into that Johnny Walker."

Jeb's jug ears went crimson. "Must've forgot to take my blood-pressure pills this morning."

Mace nodded. "They say the mind's the second thing to go. I forget the first."

The three chatted sparingly, trying to keep each other's spirits up, until, another hour or so later, a Somalian physician named Dr. Bashir showed up, clutching a clipboard and asking for Bella.

"That's me," she said.

The doctor, broad-browed with black-olive eyes, exuded an air of infinite patience. "I wish I had something more encouraging to tell you, Mrs. Yancy. But your husband's in a coma. His head wound is severe. The animal that attacked him must have been quite powerful. It tore into his central sulcus and parietal lobe, forming an abscess and causing his brain to swell. There's also an infection we're trying to get under control."

Dr. Bashir consulted his clipboard. "Has your husband visited any foreign countries lately?"

She looked at him dully. "The only time we've ever been out of the state was when we honeymooned in Ontario, but that was nearly ten years ago. Why?"

"It's probably nothing. It's just that his infection appears to be drug-resistant, and we wanted to rule out any foreign pathogens."

Mace cleared his throat. A terrifying idea had just occurred to him. "Could this infection be caused by a mold?"

"Mold?"

"Well, Yancy recently had a mold of some kind in his corn. Sort of rust-colored. They ended up burning the field to get rid of it."

Dr. Bashir's expression turned inward. "It's not unheard of for spores from certain molds, when inhaled, to cause brain inflammation and toxicity. I'm not familiar with any fungal infection that moves this quickly, but we can run a few more tests."

YANCY NEVER EMERGED from his coma. He died the next evening. Bella took it stoically, better than Jeb, who was the more puffy-faced and tearful of the two. Mace couldn't find any words to express his feelings. None of them had gotten more than an hour's sleep in the past twenty-four, and exhaustion compounded their misery.

One minute you're here, functioning like everyone else, and the next minute you're gone, leaving behind an empty skin suit and whatever change you've got in your pocket. Mace understood this; he'd already outlived his entire family and most of the people he went to school with. But when it came to this kind of tragedy, Yancy, just thirty-four, being taken by a monster from outer space, he had no frame of reference. His mind drifted in search of anchorage.

They drove back mostly in silence. Mace did all the driving. They stopped for gas and to use the bathroom at a Speedway station in White Bear Lake. The coffee there was an improvement over the vending-machine swill they'd been gulping down at the hospital. They loaded up on chips and candy bars, and were quickly on the road again.

Yancy's casket lowered into the ground a week later. Mace was there at the cemetery to pay his respects, as was a fair-sized assemblage of friends and relatives. Jeb, however, stayed home, feeling under the weather. Mace suspected that the whole episode was just too much for Jeb to endure any further. In the days that followed, Mace's fishing buddy kept to himself, turning into something of a shut-in.

One day, around mid-September, Mace drove his rust-bucket pickup over to Jeb's farmstead to check on his friend. Jeb met him at the screen door, standing in the shadows of the living room, scratching at himself like a dog with fleas.

"Can I come in?" Mace asked.

"Better not, kid. I've got some kind of bug that—trust me—you don't want any part of."

"Have you seen a doctor?"

Jeb blew through his lips, making a dismissive sound. "What I have, I doubt there's a cure for."

"What do you mean?"

"I got these boils on my skin that don't look like anything I've ever seen before. Itch like the dickens."

"Boils?"

"I'll show you if you promise to step back. I'm not sure if I'm contagious, but I s'pose I am."

Mace backed up a step. Jeb opened the screen door about four inches and thrust out an arm.

What Mace saw caused him to gasp. Craters of florescent red flourished like tiny volcanoes across the landscape of Jeb's forearm, teeming with furry white and green splotches and a mucusy discharge. The lesions spread across the back of his hand and to the second knuckles of his fingers.

"Holy shit, Jeb. That looks like the mold we found in the cornfield."

Jeb sighed, pulled his arm inside, and closed the door. "I think what happened was, when I fainted that second time, I cut myself when I fell, and that gave the mold a chance to enter the open wounds. It got inside me. I can feel it growing under my skin. I'm telling you, kid, it's a creepy feeling you don't want to know."

"We've got to get you to a hospital, man."

98

"I don't think so. They'll just stick me in an isolation ward where I could stare at four sterile walls until I eventually die. Naw, I'm seventy years old, I've had a good life. If I'm going to go, I'm going to go in front of my TV with a cold can of beer, watching the Vikings pound the crap out of the Packers. We don't generally get to choose how we die, but at least I can choose where."

This was a lot for Mace to take in. "Jeb, you have to see a doctor."

"I don't have to do nothing. Like that FBI lady said, it's a free country." Then, he said goodbye and closed the inside door.

Days stretched to weeks and weeks to months. Mace kept pleading with Jeb to get medical attention, but it was a waste of breath. Eventually Jeb stopped answering Mace's calls altogether and stopped opening his door when Mace knocked.

Finally, left with no alternatives, he dug out the FBI agent's card from the junk drawer in his kitchen. He got through to her at her office in Minneapolis, and told her what was happening.

"When's the last time you talked with him?" she asked.

"Maybe a month ago. He's kind of gone incommunicado."

"We'll be there in about three hours. Meet us at his farm, but, whatever you do, don't go inside his house. Just wait for us."

This time, there was no police presence, just two cars of feds and, about a half hour later, a white van with hazardous cleanup specialists. Mace and the agents put on protective suits and, with about a half-dozen members of the hazmat crew, approached Jeb's front door and knocked.

"Jeb," Mace said. "You in there?"

No answer. He tried again. Still, nothing.

"Stand back," one of the FBI agents said, and kicked the inner door open.

What met their eyes was astounding.

Inside the place, the floor, ceiling, and walls bloomed with thick patches of coppery mold. The fungus covered everything: furniture, cabinets, counters and, sitting on the couch, watching TV and drinking from a can of Grain Belt, Jeb himself. Or what might have been Jeb at one time.

Even through the coating of the mold cloaking it, they could see Jeb's body, now physically shrunken to half its normal size, was no longer draped in human flesh but in gray reptilian skin, his face a mixture of old farmer and savage beast. From the way he was leaning forward, they could tell spikes poked from his back. On the seat beside him lay a shotgun.

"I was wondering when you folks would show up," Jeb said, his voice somewhat garbled due to speaking through teeth that were now extended and needlelike. Reaching for the shotgun with one clawed hand, he put the barrel under his chin. "Here's looking at you, kid," he said, and squeezed the trigger.

COME FEBRUARY, Minnesota wore its customary coat of white. The wind picked up from the north, a chill descended, and rural denizens across the state spent as much time as they could nestled in the warmth of the indoors. Plow trucks scraped ice from the roads and schoolkids woke up early, hopeful classes would be canceled.

The government took Jeb away in one of those white plastic sacks, along with other articles from his house. Mace never heard what happened to his friend, but he assumed he was being studied in some lab somewhere. Jeb's farmhouse, having been burned to a blackened pit in the countryside, was bulldozed over, forming a gentle hill that eventually became a favorite of local snow sledders.

On clear days, Mace Stangis could still be seen occasionally puttering around the streets of Sebeka in his rust-bucket 1950 Chevy 3150, though he kept mostly to himself. Bella Yancy sold her farm and moved in with her sister Charlotte in Bemidji, but not before stopping by Mace's place to say goodbye, and for one last commiseration.

Winter, as usual, outstayed its welcome.

Mace passed away shortly before the ice began to melt. One of Herb Menshaw's boys who came over to borrow a chainsaw, found him, wearing a Vikings jersey and propped in his favorite chair, an open can of beer on the end table beside him.

Now, no one whose life had been touched by the creature from the sky was left in the area. It almost was like the whole thing never happened.

Things on the surface resumed the peaceful pace to which locals were accustomed. Below the surface, though, that was a different story.

IN THE COLD, DARK SOIL OF SEBEKA'S EVERGREEN CEMETERY, a groaning could be heard, if any ears were available and keen enough to hear it. The groan was followed by a burst of cracked wood and the hiss of rancid air releasing underground in the concrete burial vault of Bill Yancy's coffin.

Swollen beyond his casket's limits, the red mold gradually overfilled the burial vault and began leeching into the earth. It was spring before anyone noticed that the cemetery grass had taken on a coppery hue, and summer before the mold ate through the roots of the graveyard grass and began appearing on its surface.

By then, the mold had fanned out on a subterranean level through the dirt and the clay and the rocks, for miles in all directions. It began popping up as far away as Deer Creek and Backus. Government crews worked round the clock to contain it as best they could, but when it was burned to cinders in one town, it eventually showed up in another.

No mention of the red mold's extraterrestrial provenance ever appeared in the news media.

Beyond the soil contamination, the red mold entered groundwater reservoirs, affecting the drinking water in several rural towns. Officials claimed that the fungus was filtered out by city treatment centers, but even if that were true, it offered little comfort to families dependent on wells as their primary water source.

Then rumors began spreading about lizard-like creatures capable of leaping great distances that roamed the woods in search of wildlife to destroy with their pointy teeth and razor-sharp claws. But, like Bigfoot, the Loch Ness Monster, and Mothman, these reports were dismissed by most as products of overactive imaginations.

# A WORLD APART

"We are the music makers,
And we are the dreamers of dreams,
Wandering by lone sea-breakers,
And sitting by desolate streams;—
World-losers and world-forsakers,
On whom the pale moon gleams:
Yet we are the movers and shakers
Of the world for ever, it seems."
—Arthur O'Shaughnessy, "Ode"

That night, Candice Higgins, walking hand-in-hand with a Dutchman named Diederik, strolled the canals of Amsterdam. It was mid-day and, by the look of it, late autumn. Narrow Dutch homes and cobblestone walkways, teeming with pedestrians and bicyclists, lined either bank of the canal, along with leafless plane trees that reached taller than the gabled roofs of the buildings.

An empty red-and-blue sailboat bobbed at the shore near the footbridge they were crossing, and the two lovers paused to take it in, and the glittering surface of the water that held it afloat.

This was the culmination of their morning walking tour of the city. The path had wound past curious little shops with windows displaying mouse dolls or assorted neon signs or glass-boxed lizards that looked as if they might have roamed the earth in the age of dinosaurs. Past tilting structures braced from the streets with wooden beams, past tulip-lined parks and plazas, and herring carts, and the tall arched panes of churches and museums. It had been a glorious morning. It was a shame it had to end.

Even as she turned to Diederik, she could feel herself coming apart. She watched as her broad-chested beau's lucid blue eyes and blond locks began to go transparent.

"I'll miss you, Diederik," she said. "And Amsterdam, of course." She could have reached him as easily with her thoughts as with her words, but, gawd, how she loved hearing her own voice again.

"Perhaps you will return one day," he replied in his melodic Dutch accent. He leaned in to kiss her.

Then he and the entire cityscape melted away, and, once again, she lay motionless in her hospital bed staring at the stucco ceiling and listening to the occasional hiss of the ventilator that kept her breathing at night.

The door to her room opened, and utilizing the one major movement left to her, she twisted her neck.

"Good morning, Candice." It was Elmira, her Nigerian nurse. Must be six o'clock. "Did you sleep well?"

Candice clicked her tongue once. It was their shorthand: once for yes, twice for no.

"I'm happy to hear that. I also slept well." Elmira stepped to the room's window and slid open the curtains. Sunlight poured in and Elmira stood in it, assessing the view outside. "Sunny and pleasant. Just like my hometown of Abuja."

She turned and smiled broadly. One of her high cheeks carried a scar left by another patient, a psycho who'd attacked her with her own nail file right here at The Residence. Or so Candice had heard. Elmira never spoke of it. Elmira seldom spoke of anything sad.

She crossed the room to Candice and removed the ventilator mask.

"Now, let's take care of your personal needs." That meant Candice's bowel program, a task Elmira always approached with good humor, which Candice appreciated. Other nurses gave facial clues indicating their dislike of the chore, but never Elmira. She attended to poop duty

103

with the same breezy manner as she did all other aspects of Candice's quadriplegic care.

CANDICE WAS A HIGH-SCHOOL FRESHMAN when her parents died. She recalled trembling in the waiting room at North Memorial Hospital when the doctor came and told her the news. Uncle Brad, her father's brother, was there with her in his tie-dyed Buddha T-shirt and blue jeans. She watched as, behind his glasses, tears began overfilling his eyelids. Uncle Brad, stout and short with his balding pink head, hugged her tightly.

The driver of the other car was traveling too fast for the icy road conditions. He lost control of his vehicle and it leapt the concrete medium strip, crashing head-on into her family's Kia Optima. That driver died instantly, whereas Mom and Dad took hours to go.

Uncle Brad helped her with all the tough decisions regarding the funeral arrangements.

Her parents hadn't been wealthy, but they'd been middle-class wealthy, with an estate valued at two hundred thousand dollars, plus the equity in their Bloomington home, which was soon sold, the contents emptied into a storage unit where she could leisurely go through it all and decide the fates of once-treasured items. Keep this, donate that, send the rest to the landfill.

She had no idea what to do with all the money. Uncle Brad helped her with that, as well, steering her to a broker who opened an account designed to put her inheritance to work for her future.

She moved in with Uncle Brad, of course. Into the two-bedroom townhouse on Winnetka Avenue in New Hope. They'd never even discussed it. It was assumed she'd want to live with him. He cleaned out the extra bedroom for her, moved in her bed and dresser, let her decorate it as she liked. His abode was now their abode, and it wasn't long before she felt completely at home.

"I only have one rule," Uncle Brad said. "No meat in the house. You can eat whatever you like in restaurants. I'll even take you to fast-food drive-throughs. But no meat in the house."

Packages of butchered cow muscles and dissected chicken torsos upset his Buddhist sensibilities. They made him think of the painful deaths and cruelties dealt out daily at slaughterhouses.

"It would break my heart to have meat in the house," he explained.

She'd agreed to this stipulation.

Candice, then a fifteen-year-old orphan, began working her way through the stages of grief. To be honest, she and her mother had never been close, but Mom had always been around—cooking meals, doing the shopping, guiding her through menstruation and other female difficulties. Between them, though, there'd always been a gap that neither could fully breach. Mom had expectations and Candice kept coming up short.

"I see you got a B in geography," Mom would say, perusing her report card. "An A would look better when you apply for college. Small differences matter, you know."

Or, Mom would say to Dad within Candice's earshot, "She's such a tomboy. I hope she doesn't have *proclivities*." Still, Candice missed having Mom in the background.

Mostly, though, she missed her father.

Dad's temperament was halfway between Mom's and Uncle Brad's. He usually sided with his wife on matters of discipline, but when she was really worked up over some delinquency of Candice's, he'd often managed to talk her down. "She's still a kid. Why not let her be a kid for a while longer, while she still can be one?" That kind of thing.

However, when Mom dug in her heels regarding some misdeed of her daughter's, he supported her mother one hundred percent. Presenting a unified parental front was one of the few areas they wholeheartedly agreed upon.

"You're grounded one week," he would say, "for talking back to your mother." Or, "for not cleaning your room," or "for missing the school bus this morning." With him, every transgression had the same sentence: one week grounded. And once he announced her penance, he never backed down.

But it was from her dad that she learned how to patch drywall, hang a cabinet, and change a car's tire. And it was Dad who took her to see Semisonic at the state fair; who let her drive around parking lots when

105

she was preparing for her driver's test; who taught her how to ride a bike, shoot a free throw, and haggle for the best deal at a yard sale.

More than anything, she missed her dad.

Uncle Brad did his best to parent her, teaching her by example, patience, mindfulness, and the folly of attachment. Most importantly, though, he taught her how to meditate.

AFTER BREAKFAST, which consisted chiefly of soft foods (though she could technically eat anything under supervision), Candice sat in a wheelchair that she operated by puffing into a tube. Now it was her turn to look out on the beautiful morning. On sun-drenched suburbia with its newly mown lawns, asphalt driveways, shade trees, and rows of Tudor and ranch-style homes. Where normal people lived. She watched cars of middle-class moms and dads headed out for work. For the paychecks that kept the kids in braces and the debt-collectors at bay. She'd lived in the same world as these folks once. Not so long ago.

A Black teen in pigtails and rocker-chick apparel sailed down a sidewalk, legs pumping the pedals of an Ibis mountain bike. This brought Candice back to Amsterdam, where bicycles ruled the roads, and to Diederik, her shy Dutch boytoy. *Outside my night trips, when was the last time anyone had kissed me?*

That was an easy one: October 9, 2021.

A pressure ulcer on her left heel bled pus into her sock. Pressure ulcers, better known as bedsores, had plagued Candice on and off for months: on her shoulder blades, hips, tailbone, buttocks, and on the backs of her arms and legs. So far, all of hers had healed, but she knew that sometimes bedsores never did fully. And even healed ones often left scars. If bedsores got bad enough, they could even be fatal.

Eye sensors in her computer allowed her to read. Mostly she read travel books, in preparation for the nights she could leave her crippled body. She couldn't do it every night; it didn't work that way. But every night, she'd try, and nearly every night, she'd succeed.

Reading helped her prepare, though simple cyber-tripping didn't do much for her. Websites always felt truncated and incomplete. Her imagination better absorbed the richer details and insights supplied by books: travel guides, memoirs, histories.

Today, she read about Paris. Stunning Paris, the city of light. Of course, reading about a place was no guarantee that's where she'd go next, but if she packed her mind full of wonderful destinations, eventually she'd appear in one of them.

She traced the genesis of her out-of-body travels to Uncle Brad's meditation training.

Uncle Brad, of course, had never meant to teach her something that would lead her to such a profound experience as out-of-body travel. He'd never even pictured such a thing being possible. No, Uncle Brad was a disciple of Clouds in Water Zen Center in St. Paul who knew the simple benefits of going through life calmly with an unclouded mind.

"You can close your eyes or open them," he said. "Personally, I leave mine partially shut, in a sort of squint. You want to sit upright with your legs crossed and your hands resting in your lap. Relax your body and concentrate on your breath. Breathe in, breathe out. I breathe in through my nose and out through my mouth. I count my breaths to ten, then start over. When your mind pulls you away from concentrating on your breath, gently make your way back."

At first, she'd found the whole meditation thing a monumental bore. But they'd practiced together fifteen minutes a day, and eventually she began to feel the benefits from letting go of discursive thinking (what Uncle Brad called "monkey mind"). She began to look forward to their daily sessions and sometimes even meditated extra on her own.

It was during one of her solo sittings that she first experienced the amazing clarity of what Buddhists call "mindfulness." All that day, she'd carried around her newfound perspective, seeing her room, her house, her lawn, and all the outside world as if for the first time, as if blinders had fallen from her eyes. By stepping away from the chattering of her monkey mind, she entered a sense of reality both fresher and fiercer than anything she'd ever before encountered.

Initially, this new perspective frightened her, but eventually the effect became more one of wonderment.

When Uncle Brad came home from work that summer day, she told him all about it.

"Is this what they call enlightenment, Uncle Brad?"

"Some believe it is. But, in order for it to be true enlightenment, I would think it must be permanent."

"You mean it wears off?"

"Usually."

She carried it with her through to bedtime, to the fall of night and the time of dreaming.

The next morning, monkey mind was back, though to a lesser degree. It was almost a month before she again fully experienced the marvel of mindfulness.

NINE O'CLOCK rolled around at The Residence. Candice was absorbing Rick Steves' *Paris* e-guide, imagining what it would be like to idle away an afternoon at the Louvre, perusing great works of art such as *Mona Lisa* and *Venus de Milo*.

"He-lll-o-o." Katherine, her physical therapist, entered the room. Over six feet tall with a raw, chisel-boned face and springy hair, Katherine thought of herself as an angel of mercy; Mother Theresa in a vintage polyester pants suit. But Candice held her in lower esteem. "Is there much pain today?"

Her reply came in the form of a single click of the tongue.

*Being numb from the neck down should at least bring the benefit of no pain, but where's the fun in that?* Most days, she lived with searing headaches, torturous neurological distress, and when she sat up, a throbbing that slowly built in her shoulders. She'd learned to embrace all that, to "lean into the pain," as Uncle Brad had advised her that time she face-planted on the sidewalk in front of their house and ended up with six stitches.

"But it hurts," she'd protested tearfully.

"I know," he'd said, "but it will hurt less if you become one with it. Our reaction to painful situations can make things better or worse."

For the most part, he was right. He usually had been.

"So, let me tell you about *my* morning," Katherine said, as she wheeled Candice down the corridor to the rehab room. "First, my cat scratched me; clawed me, really. Left a nice, little wound on the back of my hand. But I love that cat, so what can you do? You can't reason with a cat. Then, I had to fight with my son to get him out of bed so I could take him to daycare…"

She went on and on this way, through most of the hour-and-a-half session. Through the bending and pulling and stretching and rotating. Danny, a Filipino kid who'd look almost dashing if he'd only smile once in a while, assisted Katherine and did most of the heavy lifting.

Katherine's poor-me talk exasperated Candice, who wished she could tell her to just shut up, wished she could scream, "You don't *get* to be a martyr! You haven't *suffered* enough!"

*Not like me. Not like Jeremy. Not like those other people.*

The Northeast Minneapolis bar was called The Night Before, which struck Candice as an oddly surreal name. Jeremy worked in the mailroom at Southdale Mall in Edina with a guy named Jim who played bass guitar in the Steely Dan cover band performing at the bar that evening.

The band had just begun its set when Candice and Jeremy entered and found a table near the middle of the room. She recognized the song. "Doctor Wu." Cool and jazzy with a tasteful saxophone solo. Uncle Brad had often played Steely Dan on his stone-age phonograph. She remembered that this album, *Katy Lied*, skipped during the second chorus of "Rose Darling."

Neither Candice nor Jeremy had been to this club before, but it had a sort of chic-dive quality that appealed to her. The waitresses all wore their hair up and had on miniskirts and raven-black, off-the-shoulder blouses, and the clientele consisted mostly of college-aged kids. Good thing Candice hadn't come to dance, though. The dance floor was miniscule.

"There's Jim," Jeremy said, pointing out the bass player. He nodded to Jim and Jim nodded back.

They ordered Tanqueray and tonics from a gum-chewing server.

She'd dated Jeremy long enough to consider him her boyfriend. He wasn't the sharpest tool in the shed, but he had a pleasant, easygoing nature; a handsome, lantern jaw; and pillowy Mick Jagger lips. And he was a good listener, though she wasn't sure he always followed what she was saying.

The band was midway through its third song, a rousing rendition of "My Old School," when the first gunshot rang out. Before anyone could comprehend what was going on, a second and a third shot exploded, and with them came shrieks and scurrying all around. Chairs crashed to the floor. Some people hit the deck; some scrambled for the exit.

The band stopped playing as blood blossomed on the lead guitarist's chest and he went down. A sobbing young woman with runny mascara abruptly arched backwards, then collapsed at Candice's feet.

Candice twirled to see what was going on. Three macho gangbangers were having it out, firing hot lead at one another from a distance but hitting only innocent bystanders.

*Pop-pop-pop. Pop-pop-pop.*

She turned back and met Jeremy's stunned expression. A bullet had furrowed his scalp, and as the wound overflowed with blood, he fell to his knees, his plush lips moving soundlessly. A second bullet caught him in the throat.

She whirled again toward the death dealers, anger wrenching at her gut. "You killed him! You killed him!" she howled, surging not toward the exit but toward one of the gunmen, ready to lay hands on him and tear him apart. Then everything went white. The smell of cordite smoke burned in her nostrils. She scrabbled to keep her footing, jerking again and again, before tumbling into oblivion.

FROM TEN-THIRTY TO NOON, they left her alone at The Residence, unless she had an appointment with one of the endless stream of faceless doctors who came to call on her. But their visits had become rarer as time marched on. Sometimes they went a whole month without pestering her.

This morning she returned to her e-book on Paris. In her mind, she was standing at the latticed base of the Eiffel Tower, built in 1889 to celebrate the one-hundredth anniversary of the French Revolution. Over a thousand feet tall, it took more than two years to complete, and was hailed by many as a climactic moment of the industrial era. For a few francs, guests could climb the structure by stairs or by elevator. (Candice imagined she'd take the stairs because, hey, it's the Eiffel

Tower and she wanted to climb it.) The view from the top was breathtaking.

Next, she toured the Rodin Museum with its brilliant plaster and bronze sculptures, such as the sackcloth-garbed *Burghers of Calais*, and the study on aging titled *She Who Was the Helmet-Maker's Beautiful Wife*.

Then it was on to the Army Museum and Napoleon's tomb.

Before she'd had her night adventures to amuse her, the farthest she'd ever been from New Hope was Orlando, Florida, where her parents had brought her for a week's vacation. Her family had never been big on vacations, but Dad won airline tickets in a raffle at the American Legion, and Mom had always wanted to go to Florida, so they figured: let's go to Disney World! Despite Mom's having mother-henned her through countless queues of carousel rides and roller coasters, and meetings with strangers dressed as cartoon characters, and despite occasionally finding herself in the middle of one of her parents' quarrels, Candice, then eleven years old, had found herself swept away by the wonder and sheer majesty of the park.

She found the World Showcase at Epcot Center especially delightful, with its pavilions representing China, Morocco, Norway, and eight other foreign nations. She'd vowed to visit each one of those countries herself in actuality, as soon as she was old enough. Now, of course, she would never be old enough. Her frail body could barely handle the stress of occasional hospital visits. The only other trip she'd ever make would be leading her own funeral procession.

The rest of the day at The Residence went by with mechanical assuredness: she ate lunch, had her hair washed, read some more, received electrical stimulation to keep her muscles from losing mass, had a quick shower, and then it was back to bed for Candice.

Now, as usual, her neuropathic pain was at its peak. *Lean into it*, she reminded herself, and it helped a bit.

Sometimes, though rarely, she would have a visitor: one of Uncle Brad's friends from Clouds in Water, or a volunteer companion, or (a true anomaly!) an actual friend or relative.

This evening, Father Lipman from St. Alfonzo church stopped in briefly, offering good cheer even though Candice hadn't been a

111

congregant for years. He was the only visitor who could look at her without wincing a bit.

"They treating you alright, Candice?" the bespectacled priest asked. Sixtyish, dressed as always in his black cassock, he was almost pale enough to pass for a ghost.

She clicked her tongue once. He knew the drill. She could "talk" using her computer to supply the voice, but found the robotic male cadence off-putting, and seldom did, even though that meant leaving the conversational onus on others. Father Lipman, though, didn't seem to mind. He was chatty enough for the both of them.

"Do you feel like having company?" he asked pleasantly.

Again, she clicked.

He told her a joke about a grasshopper who came into a bar. "The bartender said, 'Do you know they named a drink after you?' And the grasshopper replied, 'You mean they named a drink *Howard*?'" The priest's piercing blue eyes sparkled.

He talked about the new organ the church was getting, about a pleasant walk he'd had that morning, about his head usher's lovable English sheepdog, and other light topics. Then he gently squeezed Candice's deadened shoulder and said, "Be well, my friend." And he was off, somehow having taken the edge from her bitterness.

The Filipino kid showed up later with a tray of veggies and some kind of rice dish that he spoon-fed her.

After dinner, she read some more about Paris until her eyes were too tired to read, then she watched a Netflix show about a blind girl and her friends who were solving a crime. Then she meditated, which helped her prepare for her night's journey.

The first time she left her body, she'd been immersed in deep meditation. She'd slipped into mindfulness, and then ... then emerged into a whole new world. Accidently, no less.

Not sure what she'd done or how she'd done it, she stood with pristine white-gloved hands folded, in a queue of pristine white-dressed children making their way to the front of a church. St. Alfonzo's! She hadn't been to mass since grade school, but here she was, not dreaming it but living it (or, rather, reliving it) as a second-grader at her first communion.

The only things whiter than the children's garb were the chunky legs of Arminda Larch, who stood directly in front of her.

From the head of the line came the words, "the body of Christ."

Then she blinked her eyes, and she was back in the living room of her and Uncle Brad's duplex, not frightened but exhilarated; wanting to do it again; to return and see where it would lead; the memory still crisp in her mind, crisp as the folds of her communion dress.

It took her more than two months to duplicate the experience, though the next time took her to the public pool in Plymouth, where her father bounced her up and down in the water, and she giggled.

Gradually, by trial and error, she developed a mindful routine that sometimes allowed her to will herself from her body. She gained some control over the experience, systematically bending it to her wishes. She couldn't control where she went, but once she was there, she could control her own reactions and bits and pieces of her virtual environment. And she could influence her destinations by reading about exotic locales ahead of time, and could usually at least project herself from her body and go *somewhere.*

When she got there, wherever *there* was, it would be far from her life as a scrawny orphan whiling away the hours in New Hope, Minnesota.

Back then, she never guessed how valuable this ability would one day become.

Now, in her hospital bed in The Residence, a night-shift caregiver arrived at nine-fifteen to check on her and turn out the lights.

Closing her eyes, she focused on the darkness of the room beyond her lids. Once she could see it clearly, her essence began to faintly vibrate. She relaxed. Now the vibration was accompanied by a buzzing and a sensation like a mild electrical shock. The trembling grew into waves that gently lapped from her head to her feet.

She felt herself hollowing out.

Slowly, she took charge of the tingling feeling and the lapping waves, at length, speeding them to a continuous hum and flow that allowed her to wedge firmly into that gray region between consciousness and sleep. She stretched, and felt her essence rub against the confines of her body.

This was as far as she'd gotten her first few attempts: moving her inner being within her frame but not beyond it. She'd been too eager, attempting to force things. She'd gradually learned that entering this phase required great equanimity and patience. But, even in her failures, her awareness grew. As did her determination.

Now she concentrated, first on her feet, swelling them then diminishing them. Expanding them into giant clown feet, reducing them back to normal size. Next came her head, which she elongated several inches in all directions, before snapping it back to its given shape and stretching it again. Once her head and feet pulsed in unison, she extended and contracted her shoulders. Now the buzzing became more of a whine, and the waves began violently rocking her.

Dizziness swept her. In the darkness beyond her lids, she sensed the approach of an awakening.

Suddenly, her field of vision expanded, exploding in a quavering spectrum of color. All at once, she fell, she floated, she was weightless. The whining became a deep-throated drone. The mild electrical charge morphed into brilliant strobe lights, and the colors became shapes and patterns that spun and overlapped and vanished as soon as they each appeared.

Then she was out, bursting into her dark room at The Residence, looking down on her useless form as she rose higher, watching herself shrink smaller and smaller till she and her bed and her imprisoning little room disappeared entirely—and she was once again free! Free to scratch her chin and curl her toes, to dance and sing songs, to breathe without effort. Free from the pain and the loneliness and the boredom.

Free from the miseries of her life.

WHEN SHE AWOKE, she still felt the warmth of Nassau's sun on her face. Felt the gentle grit of fine sand between her toes. On the harbor, while sipping a fruity rum concoction and wearing a poinsettia behind one ear, she'd looked out on a trail of commercial ships that stretched to the horizon. She'd island-hopped in a glass-bottomed boat, explored the tunnels and dungeons of ancient Fort Charlotte, strolled through colorful Parliament Square. Scarlet poinciana trees and purple bougainvillea lined the streets, and the air was fragrant with tropical roses.

But she had little time to bask in the glow of her island adventures before she suddenly became aware that, in the real world, something was wrong.

The stucco ceiling had mutated into ivory cork-board panels. Her ventilator had developed a brassy, industrial tone. Her eyes moved freely left and right, but half her face felt like a lump of clay. Unfamiliar faces hovered over her.

One of them, a doctor, was speaking. "…an ischemic stroke, which interrupted the supply of blood to your brain. You're in the intensive care unit at Methodist Hospital where we can closely monitor your condition. We've given you heparin, which is an anticoagulant, and started you on clopidogrel, which is an antiplatelet drug. We must be very careful with you, obviously, because your quadriplegia is a serious complication. Do you understand?"

She clicked her tongue once.

The face smiled thinly. "Good. Get some rest, and I'll be back to check on you in a bit."

Now only one face remained hovering: a woman's face, looking concerned.

A straw appeared in Candice's periphery and she sucked water through it.

"Would you like me to turn on the TV?" the face asked her.

THE COMBINATION OF THE MEDICINE and the aftershock of the stroke had her drifting restlessly. Memories and fantasies interwove with fragments of wakefulness. Worried eyes above watched as she pirouetted through the bamboo forest of Kyoto, Japan. The pirouette became a waltz and her dance partner was Uncle Brad, bald-headed and grinning goofily, as the forest transformed into the red sand dunes and lanky trees of the Namib Desert. Aside from the smile, Uncle Brad looked pretty much the way he had that day his heart gave out, sending him (hopefully) into rebirth and a whole other life. *How I miss him.*

Rectangles of pearly light shot through the night sky as she roamed among the quartzite sandstone pillars of Wulingyuan in south central

China. The amplified sound of her breathing chased her into the sky as a hot-air balloon lifted her into clouds over the rock-carved city of Cappadocia, Turkey. Far below, her parents waved to her. *Hi, Daddy! Thanks for all that money! Too bad I had to give it all to doctors and caregivers.*

Shrieking beeps ruptured her dreamworld and she tumbled, head over heels, into a familiar blackness. It was exactly like that split-second when she'd been meditating in the living room of her duplex, about to accidently stumble out of her body the first time. Only now the in-between chasm went on and on. Here and there, juddered faint images like ghostly jellyfish. Elmira smiling pleasantly with sponge in hand; Mickey Mouse at Disney World; Diederik, her imaginary Dutch lover, leaning in for a kiss; Jeremy doing his final, jerky dance steps. She kept expecting to escape into her other world. Like always.

But, instead, as the beeping flattened to a steady tone, her essence rode a tidal wave of numbness and total darkness that churned ever faster. Her astral ankles and knees loosened, and her spectral bones and flesh commenced lengthening. Her arms and elbows uncoupled from their joints. The vertebrae of her spine clacked like castanets. Longer and longer, she continued to stretch painlessly, all the while languidly squirming like some unicellular organism viewed through a microscope. Her head watched as the rest of her body vanished into the void until the force that drew her left her taut and spaghettified.

Her sentience began shuttering down like a series of windows, one by one, most going light-tight and black, though a few allowed the merest sliver of glow to escape. From somewhere in the dark, she felt the eyes of millions upon her.

Her particles became unentangled and broke away in pairs. Some of them continued the plunge, some fell off and drifted like dandelion spores into the vast, surrounding planes of emptiness she now recognized as her universe. And that recognition…

That was the last thing she ever perceived.

# ELLIOTT'S JUST DESSERT

"The sin which is unpardonable is knowingly and willfully to reject truth, to fear knowledge lest that knowledge pander not to thy prejudices."
—Aleister Crowley, *Liber Librae*

## 1.

The waspish older man in the long jacket waited impatiently on the bridge near the garden's orange-and-white Bentendo building. He was of average height, and even from a distance, Elliott Worley could see he had a sunken, unpleasant face and a demeanor to match. As he neared him, the figure clenched his jaw and regarded Elliot with the eye of a hungry vulture.

"Mr. Mallock?" Elliott asked hesitantly.

"I don't like waiting," came his reply. "You're ten minutes late."

Elliott detected a trace of a Gaelic accent. Well, the old-timer certainly looked his part.

"I'm sorry. Got held up in traffic. I appreciate you meeting with me."

The old man grunted.

It was the first cool day in September, coming after more than a month of temperatures in the eighties and nineties. A reprieve, that's how Elliott saw it; not quite sweater weather, but close. For others, it was the first gray glimpse of the coming tsunami known as Minnesota winter.

They followed a tar path out and around a central pond, the codger walking heavily as if carrying a great weight on his shoulders. There was no one else in the Bloomington garden at this early time.

"Are you a superstitious man, Mr. Worley?"

"Um." Elliott thought for a moment. "You mean, do I believe in ghosts?"

"In ghosts, karma, fortune-telling, demons." He paused for a moment to take in the beauty of the Japanese garden's pruned greenery. "Do you believe in a supreme deity who holds the dead accountable for things they did while living?"

"Um, are you asking me if I'm religious?"

"Yes, that's what I'm asking. Do you consider yourself a religious person?"

Elliott gave the question a pleasant frown. He raised his eyebrows and nodded. "Well, I was raised Lutheran, if that's what you mean. I don't go to church anymore, but I have nothing against it. As far as God goes, well, they say God is love, and I believe in love, so I guess I believe in God."

"And the afterlife?"

"Who knows? Do I think angels will greet me at a golden gate? Probably not. Will my psychic energy continue to exist in some form? Maybe."

Mallock tapped his front teeth thoughtfully with a fingernail, as if considering Elliott's answers.

"You asked for this meeting, Mr. Worley," he said, resuming his lumbering pace. "I assume you have something specific in mind?"

Elliott cleared his throat. "Yes. Well. I was told you perform a certain ritual. For a fee."

"Who told you this?"

"A friend of my wife's. I'd rather not say."

"Does your wife's friend live on University Avenue in St. Paul? Does she have a sign on her lawn that says, 'Fatima sees all. Consult the spirits, consult the stars?'"

Elliott's eyes fluttered.

"Relax, Mr. Worley. Your wife's friend is my friend, as well. One of my very few friends, I might add. She told me you might be contacting me. Go on with your story."

"My Great Uncle Rory, Rory Gargery, my mother's uncle, originally came to this country from the Scottish Highlands. A place called Dourgeldie. Ever hear of it? It doesn't matter. Anyway, Uncle Rory's family, now *there* was a superstitious bunch."

They approached a waterfall, its cascading waters providing a peaceful opus.

"The Gargerys believe in what you do. Sin eating, they called it. They believe that certain people—people such as yourself—can remove from the dead all culpability for past misdeeds, ensuring the deceased entry into heaven. Do I have that right?"

Mallock's lips twitched with amusement. "Go on."

"Well, the Gargerys, at least the ones on my mother's side, have all died, except for Uncle Rory, who has amassed a meager estate that, upon his death, would pass to me, provided a sin-eating ceremony be performed on his corpse prior to burial. Otherwise, the money will go to a Scottish orphan fund."

"And we wouldn't want that, would we, Mr. Worley?"

Elliot wasn't sure how to take that comment, so he let it pass. "Um, anyway, if you'd be willing to perform the ceremony, I could give you a slight stipend. Say, a hundred dollars."

"You ask me to take upon my mortal soul the lifetime of sins belonging to a man I don't even know, and you offer me a hundred dollars? I'm afraid you'll have to do better than that."

Elliott winced, shut one eye, and wiped his mouth. His voice was little more than a whisper: "How much?"

"Ten thousand dollars."

He gasped. "Are you serious? Ten thousand dollars to perform an absurd…"

The old man's vulture eye sparkled. "That's my price, Mr. Worley. Take it or leave it."

Elliott groaned. "For that kind of money, I should do it myself."

Mallock grinned. "I'd advise against that. You have no idea what you'd be getting into."

"Would you take two hundred?"

Mallock smoothed a wrinkle from his jacket. "Good day, Mr. Worley. Call me should you feel more magnanimous."

The sin-eater slowly turned heel and trudged off toward the garden entrance.

ELLIOTT PRESSED HIS WIFE, Willa, for someone less pricy to perform the ceremony. She, in turn, pressed her friend Fatima, who asked around but came up empty. Mallock was the only sin-eater in the entire Midwest, as far as anyone knew.

"Guess you'll just have to pay the guy what he wants." Willa, thin-hipped and freckled, with blue-tinted hair and a recessed chin, crossed her arms as if the matter was settled.

"Ten thousand is just too much. Hold on, maybe we can hire someone to pretend to be a sin-eater. Who'd ever know the difference?"

"Who do you know that's willing to do something like that, babe? Eat food off a dead man's chest; isn't that what you said a sin-eater does?"

Among other things. "But it's silliness. Superstition. Dead is dead, and sin and the afterlife are just inventions to get people into church pews."

"You sound pretty sure of that."

"I am."

"You sound as if you might even consider doing it yourself."

"I am considering it."

Willa's eyes enlarged. "If you do, I won't be there. I don't want to watch it. I refuse to have that memory of you in my head. I don't even like thinking about it."

Ultimately, Elliott called back Mallock and agreed to his full fee. He wasn't sure how much Uncle Rory's estate was worth, but there was a house involved and investment accounts, so taking a ten-thousand-dollar hit on the inheritance might not be so bad. And it would genuinely honor his uncle's wish.

Still, it steamed him that Mallock was unwilling to come down even a penny on his ridiculous asking price—the greedy old bastard.

During the next few months, Elliott let his unhappiness over the sin-eater and the ten-thousand-dollar expense fester. Mallock was nothing but a conman who put on a charade to take advantage of the weak-minded and the gullible. How many sad souls had he fleeced over the years?

The horrid swindler was due a comeuppance, and Elliott decided he'd be the one to finally deliver it.

UNCLE RORY HUNG ON till January before giving up his ghost in the cardiac unit at North Memorial Hospital in Robbinsdale. The phone call came the morning after from Dickenson Funeral Home in New Hope. The mortician, a Mr. Avery, having expressed his sorrow for Elliott's loss, said he understood a religious service would be conducted before the embalming, and that the ceremony needed to be arranged quickly.

Elliott contacted Uncle Rory's solicitors, Helmuth and Marley, who would send a representative to witness the ceremony and ensure it was all aboveboard.

Then he called Mallock.

"Do you think we could invite Fatima, as well, babe?" Willa had asked, pursing her lips in a way that raised her sunken chin. "I think she'd love to see something like this."

"Um, well, we don't want this thing getting any bigger than necessary. Why don't you just record it on your smartphone? That way, you can show it to anyone you like."

The Worleys arrived at the mortuary at twelve sharp. Mr. Avery, a suitably somber and sympathetic middle-ager in what appeared to be a toupee, met them at the entrance and escorted them to a windowless steel door on the basement level where Janna Higgins, a silver-haired paralegal from the law firm, awaited them, wearing a polyester pantsuit and aviator-style eyeglasses. She offered firm handshakes and tried to look calm and professional, but Elliott could see anxiety churning behind her façade.

Avery's phone rang, and he excused himself to greet Mallock, who'd just arrived.

"Ever been to one of these before, Janna?" Elliott asked.

She shook her head.

"Neither have we, but we hired a professional to conduct the ceremony, and I'm sure it will go just fine." But even as he said this, unease crept upon him.

She nodded, the corners of her eyes crimped, her lips dry and bloodless.

Mallock, accompanied by Avery and carrying a worn black satchel, arrived in the corridor looking more like an undertaker than the mortician himself. The old man wore a black suit, black shoes and tie, and a shirt as white as a moonlit sail. His hollow face grim, his jaw clenched, he turned his hungry eye at once on Elliott and nodded to him warily.

Avery unlocked the metal door, activated fluorescent ceiling lights, and ushered them in.

The embalming room was maybe eighteen feet wide and slightly deeper, the floor tiled in white linoleum squares, the walls painted a somber dun. Enameled cabinets, a sink, and assorted instruments and machinery gave the room a crowded appearance. A second door (presumably to a storage room) beckoned from a far corner. But Elliott's attention immediately sprang to the sheet-covered form on the brushed-metallic prep table in the chamber's center. Uncle Rory.

In many ways, Elliott's only connection to him was by blood. He'd appear occasionally at a Worley holiday dinner, a vaguely sinister character with a gin-blossom nose and boozy, covetous eyes, who spoke very little and never directly to Elliott.

"Be careful around your uncle," Dad would warn him whenever Uncle Rory was coming around. "He may be family, but that doesn't mean you should trust him."

Now, in the embalming room, Mallock set down his bag and turned to the assembled. "All of us are sinners. We live life by trial and error, and sometimes we stumble. We're told that our creator will forgive us all, but will he really? Will he forgive us for everything? If that's the case, explain the multitude who sizzle in Hades' lake of fire. No, our god may love us, but not unconditionally. In the end, he will judge us, and who among us will stand confident of entrance to his holy realm when his penetrating vision has examined us to our very core?"

Everyone present, except Elliott, visibly shrank under the power of Mallock's gaze.

"What I do today, my people have done for thousands of years. By taking this man's sins upon me, I wipe his slate clean. Every lustful thought, every shameless lie, every transgression that he has committed since the day of his birth, I will take upon myself and carry to the day I die. And his soul will be without blemish in the eyes of his god."

He smiled an awful smile that triggered cringes all around.

With that, the sin-eater turned and ploddingly approached the corpse. As the others amassed at a closer but still respectful distance, he methodically folded back the sheet from Uncle Rory's face, clear to his naked midsection. Pallid, pimpled, and sprouting tufts of mouse-colored body hair, Uncle Rory looked as if *his* last meal had been a particularly unpleasant one.

Mallock mumbled in Gaelic over the cadaver and gestured with one hand, then he turned to his satchel and opened it. He removed a fringed black stole with embossed symbols. He kissed this before setting it on his neck. Next, he produced a cracked, gold-rimmed saucer that could have been a museum relic. Ogham script divided the plate in half, and the halves displayed fire-belching griffins that faced one another. He placed the saucer squarely on Uncle Rory's matted chest.

Next, he removed a beige cardboard box that contained a thick slice of chocolate cake with chocolate icing. He set the pastry on the saucer and, after licking frosting from his fingers, returned the box to his bag. He took out a leather pouch, opened its throat, pinched out some granular substance—maybe salt or sugar—and sprinkled it over the cake. Then he took out a bottle of Dark Island Ale and passed it back and forth over Uncle Rory's mortal remains, again whispering Gaelic words. He opened the bottle and drank its contents dry.

For an instant, Elliott thought he saw Uncle Rory stir. Must be a trick of the light.

Then the sin-eater lifted from the saucer that substantial slice of chocolate cake, careful to get every crumb of it. He turned to the gathering and before their startled eyes opened wide his jaws and, using both hands, forced the whole portion into his mouth. His cheeks bulged.

Stuffing in so large a piece reddened his face and quickly cast a glaze over his eyes.

"Goodness!" Willa dropped her smartphone to the floor. "He's choking!"

But nobody moved to assist him. Instead, they watched aghast as the sin-eater forced his teeth through that great mouthful of chocolate confectionery, his head bobbing and twisting with the effort, the veins of his temples straining. He chomped, gagged, and chomped some more.

Gradually, his tongue was able to force some of the sodden sweetness down his throat. His coloring slowly returned. He chewed with renewed assurance until the last of the cake was gone.

Then, once again, he pivoted to Uncle Rory and, to the horror of all, kissed the dead man full on the lips.

Elliott was unsure how Mallock pulled it off, but somehow, the charlatan made the corpse shudder beneath him. As the sin-eater pressed lips to the cadaver's cold flesh for what seemed an eternity, the dead man's shoulders bucked as if attempting to expel something deep within.

Janna swooned. Avery sobbed. Elliott stood frozen in amazement at the old man's skillful deception.

Now, the corpse seemed to resume its interrupted slumber, and Mallock separated himself from what was surely the foul taste of those horrid lips. When he faced the assemblage for the last time, he had visible foam on his mouth, the origin of which was never questioned or explained. He looked upon their shaken countenances in serene triumph.

Elliott, holding a shivering Willa, broke the silence: "Is that it?"

"The ceremony is ended," Mallock said, returning the black stole and the saucer to his satchel. He recovered Uncle Rory's face with the sheet, then said, "All that remains is to collect my fee."

"Um, sure." Elliott pulled from his coat pocket an envelope containing the check. "Here you go, Mr. Mallock. Thanks for your services."

The sin-eater looked at him sharply, the vulture eye ignited with piercing malevolence. His ancient eyebrows bunched, his foam-ringed mouth set in a grimace, then, as all watched, Mallock took the envelope, picked up his bag, and tromped from the room.

IN COMING DAYS, Elliott took possession of Uncle Rory's money and assorted worldly goods, and the total amounted to something north of three hundred thousand dollars. He almost felt bad for Mallock, having handed the grifter a check drawn on a bank account closed a half dozen years ago. He expected a belligerent phone call from the old fool, but none ever came. If it had, Elliott was prepared with a simple response: "Sue me."

He chuckled at the thought of the decrepit imposter explaining to a judge that Elliott owed him ten thousand dollars for consuming chocolate cake in the basement of Dickenson's Funeral Home. At that point, Mallock would be lucky not to be hauled to a state hospital.

Willa, upon learning from Fatima that Elliott had paid the sin-eater with a rubber check, fumed. "How could you, babe? How could you cheat that poor man? Fatima is beside herself, having recommended us to him. She even offered to pay his fee herself, but he refused."

"Um, well, I gave him a chance to lower his charge. If he comes down to, say, two or three hundred dollars, I'll still pay him. Otherwise, as far as I'm concerned, he can go whistle."

"Oh, Elliott, I hope you know what you're doing."

Weeks passed, and, having heard nothing from the stiffed charlatan, Elliott assumed that was the end of it.

But then, on a blustery February afternoon, in the parking lot of Cub Foods in Maple Grove, a half-frozen Elliott was scampering past a chest-high mound of plowed snow toward the store's entrance when who should appear from out of the cold, but the hollow-faced old sin-eater himself?

Wearing the same long jacket he'd worn when Elliott had first met him in the Japanese garden months before, and carrying the black bag from the ceremony in the embalming room, Mallock stood stone still, blocking Elliott's way. The glare from his wicked eye seared with awesome intensity.

"Um, listen, Mallock," Elliott said, holding up his hands, "I'll pay you three hundred dollars, which I think is more than..."

The sin-eater was having none of it. He dropped the satchel in the snow at his feet and, with a rage that bordered on the demonic, seized Elliott by the ears and pulled his terrified face within inches of his own.

"Ow! Ow! What are you doing?"

"Since you have chosen to defraud me of my pay, I choose to give something to you."

"Ow! Wh-what do you mean?" Elliott tried pulling back, but the old man had his ears in a clench of iron.

"You think you know what my services are worth? Well, judge for yourself. Every sin of your uncle's that I took upon me, I give to you, along with the sins of the countless others I've collected over the years. *Bealach millidh ort!*" And with a great roar, he bellowed his steaming, fetid breath into Elliott's open mouth.

Elliott staggered as a deluge of transgressions and depravities howled into his being, threatening to burst him at the seams. Memories of murders, arson, thefts, rapes, and scenes of hideous torture overwhelmed his brain. Quivering abductees, weeping children, those left destitute, those left crippled and maimed, bullet-riddled corpses, these images that hundreds of sinners once carried as tokens of their sordid past deeds took shape in his heart, along with the knowledge that ownership of these crimes now darkened his conscience. And the ghastly visions kept coming—multiplying and melding into a putrid stew of shame and sorrow, remorse and disgust. Never before had Elliott found himself choking back self-hatred so rabidly. And all for sins he did not even commit.

When, at last, Mallock let go of him, Elliott stumbled backward and landed heavily on the snowy surface of the parking lot. He fell to an elbow and looked up woozily. The sin-eater's smiling face swam in an awareness that no longer belonged solely to Elliott but was now shared with myriad presences.

He rose groggily to his feet with the assistance of a concerned passerby. In the innocent eyes of the teenaged Good Samaritan, he saw reflected a figure he barely recognized. Elliott shook his head, trying to clear it, but the weight of all that had entered him left him sluggish.

"You alright, friend?" the young man asked.

Elliott tottered on his heels. He looked into the youngster's face in hopes of getting another glimpse of himself but instead focused on the countenance of his helper, on the altruism and naivety shining from the boyish face: traits that Elliott suddenly found revolting. He fought the urge to attack this benevolent creature, to knock him bloody to the pavement and corrupt him in a dozen vile ways.

Shuddering and pushing the youth away roughly, he stumbled like a drunkard to one of the cars parked nearby and rested heavily on its fender.

In the distance, he saw Mallock carrying the black satchel, walking into the store with a newfound lightness in his step.

### 2.

He searched for the sin-eater in the aisles of the market, drawing unwanted attention from the other shoppers. They gawked at him, flinched from his gaze, cringed from his path. Through the fresh fruits and the delicatessen, down rows of canned vegetables and boxed instant meals, past shelves of sweet and salty snacks, he hunted for the old bastard.

When he came to a lane of glass-encased frozen foods, he suddenly stopped. Regarding him from a frosty, mirrorlike pane was the same wretched image he'd glimpsed in the teenager's eyes but large as life, and he studied it in disbelief. It was a poor likeness of the face that had stared back at him from the shaving mirror just this morning. His features were now gray and crudely drawn, pasted with a hateful grimace and lurid eyes, his frame oddly twisted, his fingers curled like the limbs of a lifeless oak. He radiated the loathing for all humanity that burned in his now-blackened heart.

"Can I help you, sir?" A store worker, looking alarmed, hesitantly approached. Her *May I Help You?* badge read: BERENICE. Barely past puberty, stocky and rosy-cheeked in bubblegum-pink hair and movie-star eyeglasses, she seemed too young to hold a daytime job.

Again, the urge to do malice arose in him. He wanted desperately to wrap his clawlike fingers around her fat neck and squeeze. Squeeze until she colored and gaped at him. Squeeze until she weakened, and he

127

could feel the life draining from her. Till her eyes went blank and starry, and he could relish the scent of the last breath escaping her lips.

Gesturing wildly, he awkwardly fled, past startled hovering faces, between pushed wire carts, down waxed tiles that had his feet slipping, and slabs of milky overhead lights that glowed down at him like train lights in a fog. A sharp corner nicked his knuckles. If the exit doors hadn't opened automatically, he would have crashed through the glass to escape.

Faltering into the wind-whipped parking lot, he tripped to one knee, lost a shoe, got back up, and zigzagged desperately, searching out his car. A spooked soccer mom loading groceries into her trunk looked up at him, panicky. By the time he located his vehicle, an icy chill knifed at him, and it wasn't the weather alone that caused it.

He flung open the door and slid into the relative warmth.

Shivering, he started the engine, watched the defrosters go to work on his clouded windshield, rubbed his shoeless foot. Then, a terrifying vision confronted him in the rearview mirror: the shifty, glistening, maniacal eyes of a psychopath leering back at him.

The image sickened him.

What was it that Elliott's father had told him? *We are what we do.*

Whenever Elliott was caught in a lie, or brought home from school a poor grade, or misbehaved in some childish way, he was faced with his father's disheartening countenance, voicing that simple phrase: "We are what we do, son. If you want to be a good person, do good things."

Now, burdened by the guilt of a thousand sinners, it was too late to do good things. The memories of all that depravity had imprinted on him a wickedness nearly impossible to contain.

He thought again about the soccer mom he'd just startled in the parking lot. How good it would feel to grab her by the hair, not to force himself on her or pummel her, but to feel the follicles gather in his fist, straining from her scalp, her glorious screams swelling in the wind.

He spun out of the lot, the giddiness of his imagined attack arousing him.

A drink. That's what he needed. Find a bar, down some shots, and calm himself, if only a bit.

He turned onto Weaver Lake Road, remembering there was an Applebee's there somewhere.

Three minutes later, a waiter showed him—stormy-eyed and still missing a shoe—to a back booth, where he ordered two double whiskeys and a beer chaser. He avoided all customer sightlines, not wanting to get any more ideas. Instead, he stared at the tabletop, drinking sullenly.

*I just need time to think. To sort things out.*

That was the plan, anyway.


HE TORE THROUGH THE BARE ROSE BUSHES and skidded his car to a halt on his snow-crusted front lawn. Despite the sudden stop, the fluids in his head and belly continued to whirl. The smell of burnt rubber assailed him.

As his equilibrium returned, he considered staying where he was, sleeping in his car for the night. It beat having to explain himself. And it meant Willa would probably be safe from the threat posed by his newfound sadistic impulses. There was also the added plus of possibly succumbing to hypothermia. He'd heard that was a peaceful way to go.

Outside, night had fallen, leaking only whispers of moonlight through a dark overcast. Since this afternoon, the temperature had nosedived into almost-unbearable territory, but at least the wind had died down. Still, no living thing roamed the streets. It was too cold even for the rabbits and squirrels.

Thoughts of his own mortality had been ebbing and flowing in his head since this afternoon at Applebee's, mixing into a dark cocktail with the dreadful memories, the urges to batter harmless humans senseless, and the deepening suck of the liquor.

At the restaurant, an acne-faced manager with moussed blond hair (when had tenth-graders started taking over the customer-service field, anyway?) with a *May I Help You?* badge that read: BRIAN came to his table to inquire about his well-being.

"I'm fine, Brian. Just had a rough day." *And the only thing that would make it better was if I savagely rammed this tabletop ketchup dispenser into your eye.*

"How much have you had to drink, sir?"

129

He looked at the empty jiggers of whiskey and the half-finished beer before him. "A little."

"Well, you're looking like you've had more than a little. I've told your servers that you've reached your limit. Maybe it's time to head home."

Everyone in the restaurant was staring.

Rage must have flashed in Elliott's eyes because Brian, open-mouthed, took a half-step back and added, "After you've finished your beer." He leaned forward and set the bill on the table.

Elliott grunted and looked away. Imagining Brian with an eyeful of Heinz, he drained the beer, paid up, and left.

Next stop: MGM Wine and Spirits, where the salesgirl, eyeing him like he was homeless, sold him a fifth of Glengarry Highland Scotch. Then he swung through a drive-through, bought a Coke, poured out half of it, and filled the cup back up with the scotch. And off he went, destination: nowhere in particular.

He took to the freeways, the highways, and the city streets, driving out as far as the Mall of America in Bloomington and Target Field in downtown Minneapolis before circling back to New Hope, never getting out of the car, just riding, steering and drinking, pausing now and then in parking lots when his sight got too blurry. He remembered thinking, *Maybe this is a good day to die behind the wheel.*

Now, in his front yard, the porchlight blinked on, and Willa in an unzipped parka stepped from their home. "Elliott?" she asked, vapor curling white from her lips.

He staggered out onto the lawn. Neighbors flocked to windows to discover what caused this commotion. Across the street, Bruno Stangis, the neighborhood loony, stood in an open doorway, silently watching. Elliott flipped him off.

In the stark porchlight, Willa trembled like a frightened doe. "Elliott, what's the matter with you? Where've you been? Are you drunk?"

Dragging his shoeless, frozen foot behind him, he plodded toward her, struggling with the crushing burden of the relic memories and villainous passions of the beings whose sins he now lugged around within him.

"Ran into Mallock," he said, slurring his words. "The old bastard. Let me tell you, when it comes to retribution, nothing beats the payback power of a sin-eater." His chuckle verged on a moan.

"Let's get you inside," she said, rushing out to help him walk. Then, after a delay, she asked, "What happened to your shoe?"

As she led him across the threshold of their house, he bumped his hip painfully on the jam, and the vengeful hatred once again barreled up in him. He flung her aside, nearly upending her. She stared at him, a flicker of fury crossing her features. The battle to hold back his stupefying wrath had him tremoring. *Mustn't hurt Willa. Mustn't hurt Willa.* He waved away the surge of rankle that threatened to encompass him and, heaving past her, crashed onto the sofa.

Willa raked back her blue-tinted hair and observed her husband. "What did Mallock *do* to you?"

"He bestowed his sins on me!" Elliott said, drawing out his syllables.

"Sins? You mean he transferred Uncle Rory's sins to you? How is that even possible?"

"How the hell should I know?" Spittle flew from his lips. "He just did! And not only Rory's sins, which are more repugnant than I'd ever imagined, but every transgression of every sinner he's ever purified. The strain of their weight is like an anchor around my neck!" His eyes teared over.

"Elliott, it's not possible." But all certainty in her voice was swirling away like bath water down a drain. "You said yourself, sin is just something churches made up to get people into the pews on Sundays."

His lips rolled back in an ugly snarl. "Yes, I did! Genius that I am. Oh, what a clever idiot I've been. I'm still unsure if there's a heaven, but I know damn well there's a hell. I'm living in it right now, in the delirium of countless evil thoughts and urges. It's all I can do to keep from smashing to pieces everything in this room. You have no idea how good that would feel."

She thought for a minute. "Let me call Fatima. She'll know what to do." Willa drew her iPhone from her back pocket and started thumbing the keypad.

He tried to follow her phone conversation with the medium, but a riptide of bleak saturninity swept him away. In visions, he saw hands

131

mechanically uncoupling tendons from bone, watched a pistol-whipping draw gushing welts of blood, saw the starved face of a young boy bloom bruises under hammering fists, heard false alibis flowing out smoothly, and the glib lies of the unfaithful reassuring weeping spouses. His fingers felt the kiss of ill-gotten coins, his ego the wash of power derived from lording over weaker wills, and on his tongue, the glorious savor of vengeance.

"He says Mr. Mallock 'bestowed' on him all the sins. Uncle Rory's and everyone else's that he had been collecting over the years. Is that possible? … I know, I know. But you should see him, Fatima. He looks like death warmed over." Willa talked with one freckled hand on the phone and the other on her hip. "Can't you talk to him, Fatima? I'm sure Elliott's learned his lesson. ... At this point, I think he'd pay Mr. Mallock *anything*, just to be rid of this curse."

She gave her husband a worried look.

Willa talked some more, but her words atrophied into a meaningless buzz. He watched her lips move. Watched her recessed chin wag. She hung up and paced the width of the living room for quite some time. His awareness slipstreamed in and out.

He must have dozed off briefly, because the next thing he knew, Willa was talking into her phone again, her face long and staid. "Yes. I'll tell him. … I understand. … I'm sure he will. Thank you, my friend. I'm so sorry we've put you through all this. … Of course. … Goodbye."

Now, Willa's image roiled as if she were on a ship in a stormy sea. He found that he could only focus one eye at a time and not for long. He rose to his elbows, but the effort was too much. He collapsed back in the sofa cushions almost immediately, looking up at her moving lips, trying to make sense of what she was saying.

"… Tomorrow morning at ten o'clock. At the garden at Normandale College where you met him before. He said to bring cash this time. You'll have to go to the credit union…"

Then her voice faded again, and he sank dully into a black and bottomless pool.

3.

Elliott hunkered on a bench outside the garden, sipping from a Starbucks cup and eyeing the students and professors who passed him on their way to morning classes. He fantasized snapping spines, garroting, raping, carving, skewering, and so on, his mind an endless wellspring of potential malaise. One of the instructors he recognized from a dark deed shared in someone else's past.

At the credit union, he'd expected to be grilled on why he wanted ten thousand dollars in cash from his savings account. He thought he might have to fill out some kind of form. If they asked, he needed the money for his brother to buy a car. But they didn't ask. The short-haired redhead in the flame-colored vest counted out the bills at the cashier's cage with casual efficiency. Almost as if the currency were worthless: Monopoly money. When she finished tallying the sum, she smiled at him and said simply, "Have a nice day."

The thick wad of cash now rested uneasily against his chest. Mallock's blood money. *Where was that old bastard, anyway?* Elliott imagined stuffing the bills one at a time down Mallock's quavering gullet. But only *after* the sins were lifted from Elliott's tortured psyche.

He recognized one of the young scholars, withdrawn and sullen, walking irresolutely by him at an edge of the procession. The image Elliott carried from the depraved mind of one of his dark passengers was of this student as a much younger boy, tearful and dirty-faced, tugging up a waistband on a pair of bloody underwear.

The tendrils of evil spread farther and wider than Elliot had ever imagined.

"How are you this fine morning, Mr. Worley?"

The sin-eater's Gaelic lilt startled him. Mallock must have stepped suddenly from a clot of jabbering students. He stood leaning forward, with hands clasped behind his back, in blue jeans and a sweatshirt, apparel that was almost festive compared to his usual dress.

"So far, I've managed to refrain from killing anyone," Elliott replied. "But if I were you, I wouldn't test that resolve."

Mallock chuckled. "Let's go for a little walk, Mr. Worley."

This time, they traveled away from the Japanese garden, around a building to a parking lot. The students out there, running late, were flying from their cars and double-timing it across the snowy tar.

"Let's get this over with, Mallock. I've got your money. You win. Now remove this blasted curse."

Mallock took the cash but ignored the demand. "Do you know how a sin-eater takes on the sins of the world without damning himself to the eternal fire? The answer, Mr. Worley, is altruism."

"Altruism?"

"Bear with me. A soldier falls on a live grenade to save his comrades. Giving up his own life for the lives of his friends. We call that altruism. A teacher steps in front of a bullet to shield her young charges from a madman's rifle attack. Again, altruism. So, what would you call it when someone willingly absorbs the sins of another so that the cleansed soul may enter paradise?"

"But the soldier and teacher don't save people for ten thousand dollars. Isn't the love of money supposedly the root of all evil?"

"Even a sin-eater needs to make a living. The powers-that-be understand that. Besides, I don't charge everyone ten thousand dollars. Just the ones who can afford to pay. Some, I don't charge anything at all. Anyway, the goodwill generated by so selfless an act as sin-eating far outweighs the minor transgression of making a few dollars on the side. That's the way it's worked for thousands of years."

Elliott grunted. He was feeling the deepening chill of winter's icy clutch. He should have worn his heavy coat. Should have worn gloves. He stomped his feet to try to generate some warmth. "Alright, let's say the sin-eater gets a pass from the grand wizard who rules over all from his throne in the clouds. What does all that have to do with carrying around the guilt and memories of countless despicable crimes? I'm not a killer, but killers' thoughts live inside me, coaxing me toward the unthinkable. How do you maintain your humanity when you've taken upon yourself so much evil?"

Mallock pulled the hood of his sweatshirt over his head. "The first thing a sin-eater learns is to compartmentalize. You put up a wall inside that separates you from all the wickedness."

"You have a wall inside you?"

134

Mallock smiled. "Not anymore. You see, now that you carry all those sins, I no longer need one. I always thought the wall would protect me from the evil, but now I know that even though it protected me from succumbing to evil's influence, still the weight of all that sin drained the joy from my life. Now, I feel reborn. Fully alive."

"What are you saying?"

"That I would not take back those sins you now carry for all the gold in El Dorado."

At first, Elliott thought he'd misheard Mallock. "What?"

"I'm not taking back the sins. That is never going to happen."

Elliott's mind went white with hatred and rage. He held out trembling hands toward the sin-eater. "Then tell me how to give this burden to someone else. Anyone else."

"I won't do that either, Mr. Worley. You're liable to pass it on to the first innocent to cross your path."

"But you have to! If you don't, I swear I'll rip you apart right here in this parking lot!" He'd said it loud enough to catch the attention of a backpack-laden Black woman in a thigh-length trench coat. But, at this point, Elliott didn't care who heard him.

"Calm down, Mr. Worley." Mallock pulled from the pocket of his sweatshirt two inches of metal handle, just enough to show he hadn't come unarmed. "I didn't say I was abandoning you. There's still a path to redemption."

Elliott gritted his teeth, struggling to hold back his fury. "Go on."

"I don't have to take back the sins to ease your burden. Nor is it necessary to unleash them on the unsuspecting. There is a third option."

MID-SUMMER BROUGHT A WAVE OF SCORCHING HEAT to the already parched Midwest. In the chapel of the Sacred Eternal Pyre Funeral Home in Black Duck, Minnesota, director Carl McNeal spoke in the soft tones of a head undertaker as he led the visitor to the open casket of the late Fionnaghal Beasley, who, at age ninety-nine, had outlived every relative short of her great-grandchildren.

"She was quite a lady," Carl said. "Well-respected and admired in her family. And by everyone else who knew her. Her parents were immigrants. From the old country."

135

One of her great-grandchildren, a beefy character with a friendly face in an ill-fitting suit, greeted the entrants with handshakes. "I'm Luther Beasley," he said. Focusing on the stranger, he added, "We're so glad you could make it. It was my great-grandmother's last wish."

Judging from her appearance, Fionnaghal had led a full and dignified existence. Her features, though wrinkled, wore an undeniable expression of matriarchal command. Her hair, colored a stern brown, was done up in a top bun. Her long-sleeved dress lay smooth upon her bosom. Her hands clasped a rosary.

Grave and taciturn, the sin-eater set down his satchel and, turning his back on the dearly departed, began, "All of us are sinners. We live life by trial and error, and sometimes we stumble…"

Yes, Elliott thought as he mouthed these words. *Sometimes we stumble.*

# HOUSE OF THE WITCHY WOMAN

"And the old Witches as soone as they heare of the death of any person, do forthwith goe and uncover the hearse and spoyle the corpse, to work their inchantments."
—Lucius Apuleius, "The Corpse Watcher"

S he was a queer old gal," Honeyboy Nils said, slipping the key into the lock and twisting. "Not in the gay sense, just odd. She was my mom's great-auntie, and when I was a kid, I'd mow her lawn for her sometimes in the summer. I guess that's why she left the place to me. One thing I remember about her was she had a wart on the tip of one finger. Never bothered to have it removed."

He turned to me. "That's strange, isn't it?"

I shrugged. "Must not have been important to her."

Freckled, with pumpkin-colored hair and a spiky beard, he nodded but looked unconvinced. "Well, maybe I got the wart thing wrong, anyway. Maybe it wasn't her who had it. It was a long time ago. Maybe I'm thinking of somebody else. I get old people mixed up sometimes.

"But let me tell you something else about the old gal I'm certain is true: her neighbors were scared to death of her. See that house across the street?" He gestured with his head.

"Yeah?"

"See that hand with the eye in the palm? Next to the front door?"

I squinted. "Yeah."

"That's what they call a hamsa. It's for protection from the evil eye."

"Evil eye?"

"It's some kind of curse. Egyptian, I think. Maybe Greek. Anyway, I know the people who live there. The Bassetts. They go to my church. And anyone who knows them knows they're not the type to give in to superstition. Normally. But when you live across the street from a spooky old hag, all bets are off. See what I mean?"

I studied the blue-painted symbol for a minute. It wasn't the sort of thing you'd expect to find on a split-level ranch house in New Hope, Minnesota. I wondered what I'd gotten myself into this time.

Not that I'd planned to help Honeyboy clean out this place. In those days, I wasn't much on planning. I just followed whatever came along. Each day began with a question mark. Each night ended with an emptied bottle. Jack Daniels if I was flush, Jim Beam Devil's Cut when I wasn't. I booked day jobs through a temp agency, did some handyman work, and picked up under-the-table cash doing almost anything else that came my way. I was dirt-poor most of the time, but at least I had a roof over my head. It was my aged mother's roof. Almost thirty years old and I was still living with my mother.

Did I mention I had no shame?

I turned back to Honeyboy, who was about to enter his late great-great-auntie's abode.

It was almost noon on a clear, late-May day, coolish but pleasant, and my thoughts mostly centered on the hundred bucks a day he'd promised me for helping him clean the place out so he could sell it. But this evil-eye talk had me a bit unsettled.

The door creaked open, letting the sun in on the otherwise dim living room.

Honeyboy, in his baggy cargo shorts, set about opening curtains.

"What was her name?" It seemed that since I was standing in her living room, I should at least know her name.

"Jolaine. Jolaine Bronski. We used to call her the Witchy Woman. If she knew how we talked about her, she would've burned this place down before leaving it to anyone in my family. To be honest, I think I was the worst of the lot. I was just a kid, but I could be pretty cutting in those days. I only mowed her lawn because she paid me."

He opened a window, letting some of the stuffiness out of the place.

138

Jolaine's living room was dusty and cluttered with creepy bric-a-brac, skulls mostly: skull woodcuts, skull art prints, skull lamps, a skull throw rug, and all manner of skull busts and figurines. Jolaine's collection included ceramic skulls, metal ones, rock ones, you get the picture, though you'd have to see it yourself to believe it.

"I take it she liked skulls." I eyed one that appeared to be the genuine article.

Besides skulls, Jolaine appeared fond of replica spiders, snakes, bats, and scary-looking dogs. A collection of other weird figurines filled a shelf: a fur-covered man-creature with horns that curled back from his head; an insane-looking old woman clutching a huge knife; menacing gargoyles; a fierce Medusa rising from a swamp. All in all, the motif of a horror film.

"When I was a kid, I had nightmares about this place," Honeyboy said.

Why did I get the feeling he'd hired me as much for my company as my cleaning prowess?

No TV, no coffee table, no sofa, nothing to remind me of any living room I'd ever seen in my life except for a decrepit, overstuffed rocking chair and a three-legged ottoman in one dingy corner. The highlight of the room was a huge pentagram, carved right into the red-oak flooring.

"What're you going to do about that?" I nodded toward the carving.

"I don't know. Maybe get someone to lay linoleum over it?"

"Or sell the place to a goth kid. I got a creepy cousin who might fit the bill."

He wet his lips with the tip of his tongue. "After we get all Auntie's junk out of here, I'm going to have to hire a handyman to do a few jobs around the place. You interested?"

"Let me think on it."

Honeyboy had rented two industrial-sized dumpsters from some junk-collection company. These sat in the driveway, lids open and ready to receive the Witchy Woman's leavings. "You sure you don't want to keep any of this stuff?"

"Uh-uh. No way am I bringing any of this crap into my house. Everything goes."

"But some of this must be worth something. You could sell it."

He shook his head emphatically. "Wouldn't wish any of Auntie Jolaine's belongings on my worst enemy. You'll think I'm crazy, but even now this stuff's giving me a creepy vibe."

Yeah, I was feeling it, too.

"Okay. You're the boss." I picked up the padded rocker and carried it out to the driveway.

That day, we cleaned out the living room, the kitchen, and one of the first-floor bedrooms. Even though the temperature was a cool sixty-five degrees, my T-shirt was soaked through with sweat by the time the sun tucked itself on the horizon.

Paying me for the day, Honeyboy said, "Can you come back tomorrow for some more of this happy horseshit?"

I stuffed the hundred bucks in my jeans pocket. "Sure. I think I can clear my social calendar. Same time?"

"Same time," Honeyboy answered, closing the door behind him, "same spook house."

THAT NIGHT, I WAS BUSHED. I gave my mom twenty bucks to play bingo at the Indian casino, finished half a carton of Ben & Jerry's Cherry Garcia ice cream, and fell asleep on the couch watching a rerun of Dateline. Spoiler alert: the husband did it.

I'm not one to remember my dreams, but the nightmare I had that night must've been pretty bad. I woke in a sweat, feeling like I'd just stepped through a giant spiderweb.

It was half past five in the morning. I made myself a cup of coffee, sat on the front steps, and watched the sun lighten the sky over New Hope. It was going to be another cold one. You could just tell.

Sipping my coffee and working a crick out of one shoulder, I thought about Honeyboy and his weird Aunt Jolaine; about the skulls and the pentagram, and the hamsa on the neighbor's house. I thought about not going back there, but a hundred bucks is a hundred bucks, and it wasn't as if I had any other prospects pounding on my door.

I showed up at around noon and was greeted by two fresh dumpsters in the driveway and Honeyboy on the threshold, propping open the front door. "Late night?"

I shrugged.

140

"What's her name?"

Married men always think single guys spend all their spare time chasing tail.

I let him have his delusions. "Names? Who bothers with names?"

He chuckled. "Ready to hit it?"

"Nothing I'd rather be doing." I never knew if Honeyboy understood sarcasm, but if he did, he didn't show it.

He motioned with his chin. "Close the door," he said. "I turned on the heat. Supposed to be in the forties today."

"Springtime in Minnesota. What can you do?"

He nodded, but I don't think he was listening. "We've got one bedroom left on the first floor. Upstairs, there's a couple more bedrooms and a second bathroom. Then, we'll check the attic. Also, there's a bunch of crap in the basement. So, if we get right to it, we'll probably be done by the day after tomorrow. Maybe the next day."

"Let's go," I said.

After a couple of hours, we'd finished work on the first-floor bedroom and on the bathroom on the second, and were taking a break. Honeyboy produced two cans of Grain Belt from a cooler in his truck.

We'd just popped them open and were sucking down the suds when a noise came from downstairs.

"Did you hear that?" he asked, looking suddenly frozen.

I'd heard the tinkling noise earlier but hadn't paid it any mind.

"Let's take a look," I offered.

Honeyboy tugged on his beard and stared at me as if he were making a life-or-death decision. "Okay," he said tepidly, and waited for me to make the first move.

From a doorway in the empty kitchen, the basement stairs dropped into darkness. A switch inside the doorway ignited a feeble yellow light that glowed on old furniture, boxes and bins, and a gritty cement floor. Down one wall ran a wood handrail. Gripping it, I led the way cautiously, testing the stairs. They held firm.

The light, insufficient for a room so large, lit stacks of paint-flaked chairs, oily cardboard boxes, and assorted machinery: a lawnmower, a snowblower, some kind of edger.

"This looks familiar," Honeyboy said, wiping dust from the lawnmower's handle.

"Ever been down here before?"

"Never. The living room entrance was as far as I ever ventured. That was scary enough for me."

It was quiet now.

Off to one side, I could make out a washer and dryer, a furnace, and a heavy-duty sink.

I started to say something else when I was interrupted by that tinkling sound again. It came from the furnace area.

"Windchimes," I said as we approached. I could see the thing dangling from a wood rafter beside a vent. "Every time the heat kicks in, the chimes jingle. Want me to take 'em down?"

"Sure. If you don't mind. That noise gives me the willies."

I was unhooking the chimes when I noticed on the other side of the furnace a doorway covered with a huge tapestry. "What's back here?"

The tapestry bore a sepia, batik-like image of a man in a dense forest bent over backward and staring at us while fighting off a buzzard or some other kind of evil-looking hawk perched on his chest. The terror on the man's face just about ate right through me.

"Oh, boy." Honeyboy's face was so drained of color I half expected him to faint.

"Let's see what's back there." I laid the windchimes on a cardboard box.

Pushing aside the covering, I felt along the inner wall for a light switch. The room was black as a coal mine, but I could sense it had some depth to it. My fingers found the switch, and the chamber flooded with light.

What I saw took the breath from me. At first, I could only stare, not believing my own eyes.

"Oh, sh-shit," Honeyboy stuttered, grabbing my arm for support. "What the holy mother of God—"

Along the far cement wall hung seven dried and petrified corpses. Men and women of assorted vintages, gnawed with rot and wearing the ghastly grimaces of death, their hollow eye sockets gawking into a netherworld only they could see. Their stony faces jutted bleakly into the light.

Each was bound to the wall with silvery wire that formed a pentagram across their chests. It was as if they'd been tied down for some ceremonial reason.

"What do we do?" Honeyboy asked.

"I don't know. Call the cops, I guess."

There's something hypnotic about corpses. I think it's because when you look into their faces, what you're really looking at is your own mortality, and if that doesn't scare the hell out of you, nothing will.

"We can't call the cops."

"What do you mean?"

"Once word got out, I'd never be able to sell this place. Who'd want to live here?"

Not me, I had to admit. "Well, you can't just leave 'em here." I took a tentative step forward, and Honeyboy followed, still hanging on my arm.

"What if we take them away somewhere? Bury them out in the woods at night or something."

"What do you mean 'we'?"

"You and me. I'd pay you, of course."

I shook my head. "There isn't enough gold in Fort Knox to get me to cart around dead bodies at night in the woods. That's not a business I want to be in. I'm more of a paint-your-house, help-you-move kind of guy."

Honeyboy toyed nervously with his beard. "You got a better idea? And don't say, 'Call the cops.'"

My personal idea was to get the hell out of there as fast as my legs would carry me. Just being in the same room with these corpses freaked the living daylights out of me. "You think Aunt Jolaine was some kind of serial killer?"

"I wouldn't have thought so. But I wouldn't have thought a lot of things five minutes ago." He let go of my arm.

I took another step closer, my curiosity getting the better of me. I studied the figure of a withered man, a spindly bag of bones whose clothes had largely disintegrated. He looked to be the oldest of the lot.

No way of telling what his age at death would have been. "Listen, Honeyboy, this is looking more and more to me like it's *your* problem. I won't say anything to anyone, as long as no one asks. But that's where I draw the line in this mess. How 'bout if you just pay me for today's work, and I go on my merry way?"

He thought for a moment, the initial shock of finding the bodies apparently beginning to wear off. "What if we buried them right here?"

"In the cement floor?"

"Yes. In the cement floor."

"Are you insane?"

"Listen. I saw it on a fix-'er-up show on PBS. They cut a hole in a cement basement floor with a circular saw. To install a sump pump. It looked pretty easy."

I couldn't decide which mental image was nuttier: Honeyboy cutting into cement with a circular saw, or Honeyboy watching public television. Still, I had to admit, maybe he was on to something. "Aren't you the least bit curious where these people came from?"

"I think I have that one figured out." He pointed to a dusty corner where a weathered wooden sign with burnt-in letters read CAT'S BACK RIDGE.

"And that's supposed to mean something?"

"A few years back, a boy went missing up north in Buena Vista State Forest outside Bemidji. They never found him, but they did find his two friends, walking along some rural highway in a daze. They had some wild tale about being attacked by a giant rock serpent or something. Anyway, I was up that way in Nebish at the time, fishing. There wasn't much about it in the news, but you know small towns, word gets around fast. And what they were saying in Nebish was that these two boys told a story about getting their truck stuck on an old logging trail, spending the night in the forest, then setting off on foot the next morning. They walked quite a ways when they came to an ancient cemetery marked with a sign—just like that one there—that said Cat's Back Ridge."

This was a lot to follow in a cement spook room with seven desiccated corpses pinned to the wall. "So, besides the sign, what's the connection? You think a giant rock serpent did these folks in?"

144

"No. But look at their clothes. What's left of them anyways. These bodies have been in the ground at least fifty years. Maybe a hundred. I'd bet anything these people were dug up from that cemetery in Buena Vista State Park and brought back here."

A chill ran through me. I was speechless. There was something to Honeyboy's tale, some element of truth that you could just sense in your bones. I looked at Honeyboy, looked at the sign, looked at the corpses.

"Maybe Aunt Jolaine heard something about these kids and their experience in the forest, and used her witchy-woman powers to track down the remote cemetery. Or maybe she knew about the cemetery all along. Either way, I'm pretty sure these bodies came from that graveyard."

"And they never found the missing dude?"

"Not that I've ever heard. They searched and searched, but that forest must be eighteen thousand acres or better. As far as I know, they never found the guy, never found the cemetery, never found the snake. Most people thought these characters were just young punks on drugs who hallucinated the whole thing. But that's not what I'm thinking."

I chewed my lip. "Okay. Let's say this theory of yours is right, and Aunt Jolaine heard about or knew about this cemetery and decided to dig up some bodies, bring them home, and hang 'em on her basement wall. That still begs the question: Why would she do that?"

Honeyboy shook his head.

"And," I added, "how could a woman seventy years old—"

"Closer to eighty."

"…Eighty years old, drive up north, travel who knows how far into the woods, dig up seven corpses from a cemetery, haul them back to her car, and drive them here?"

"She couldn't," Honeyboy said. "Not by herself."

I STILL DON'T KNOW WHAT POSSESSED ME to go back to that house. Sure, there was the money, the new amount still unsettled. (If I was going to help someone bury seven corpses in their basement floor, it was going to cost them a hell of a lot more than a hundred bucks a day.) But that wasn't the whole reason.

145

When I left Honeyboy, I'd told him I'd let him know the next day whether I wanted any part of his harebrained scheme. At the time, I was ninety percent sure I was walking away from the whole mess for good. But that night in the lamplight of my bedroom, nursing a pint of Jackie D, I found myself thinking about how, if I did help him, it'd be like embarking on some big adventure—skullduggery in the shadowy recesses of suburbia. I have to admit, it sounded a bit thrilling. Certainly, more thrilling than anything else I had going for me.

I tossed the idea back and forth in my mind until I'd wrung out all the nervous energy that had built up in my body since first seeing those emaciated carcasses glaring at me from that wall. The Jack kicked in, and I rolled off like a pinball from the flashing bumper of consciousness into the bonus hole of dreamland.

When I awoke, it was after ten. Mom was long gone to work at General Mills in Golden Valley, so I had the house to myself. I made oatmeal and a full pot of coffee, sat at the kitchen table, and listened to the chorus of songbirds outside the window. I knew what I was going to do. Apparently, in the wasteland of drunken slumber, I'd decided to take Honeyboy up on his offer.

But only if I could dictate the terms.

"Wasn't sure you were coming," he said when I showed up. He was sporting a green lumberjack shirt that hung wrinkled on his freckled arms and loudly clashed with his ginger beard.

"That makes two of us," I replied. "Let's just say I'm here to listen. If I like what I hear, then I'm with you; if not, no hard feelings, no dime-dropping, and we part as if none of this ever happened. Agreed?"

He nodded.

"First things first. Let's get the money question out of the way."

"How much?"

"How much are you offering?"

He pursed his lips. "How does a thousand sound?"

"Half sounds a whole lot better."

"Half?" He tugged on his jack-o-lantern-colored whiskers and frowned. "You mean half from the sale of the house? Come on!"

"Half for my help and silence. That's my only offer."

He made some strange faces while he worked all this out in his head. Finally, he glared at me. Then, he showed me his palms and the frown melted from his face. "Alright. Alright. Half it is. But that's for everything. For cleaning the place out, cutting the cement, burying the stiffs, and covering the floor so nothing looks hinky."

I thought about that pentagram on the living room floor. "Looks like we're going to need a lot of linoleum." I sighed. "Something else. I need you to cover up those bodies, so I don't have to look at 'em the whole time. And we should have a plan in place in case we get any visitors."

"Visitors?"

"Yeah. Like whoever helped Aunt Jolaine snatch those bodies in the first place."

"You think they'll show up?"

"They might. Why loot a cemetery, I have no idea. But they went to a ton of trouble to get their mitts on those dead folks. So, we should at least be prepared if someone shows up to claim 'em."

"But, if they take the bodies, doesn't that just solve our disposal problem?"

"Sure. As long as they never get caught with them, and they never tell anyone where they got the bodies from. Besides, do you want some gravediggers traipsing around in your house? I mean, what kind of people would we be talking about?"

"So, what are you saying?"

"We stick to the house until we get this done. Agreed?"

He looked like I just punched him in the gut. But he glumly nodded. Then we shook on it. God help us. We shook on it.

IT TOOK US THE REST OF THE DAY to get prepared.

We started by buying a cheap twelve-inch corded concrete saw. We considered renting a better one but worried that would involve paperwork and IDs, and we didn't want to leave behind any potential clues should authorities ever come asking. We bought a couple of finishing trowels, two sixty-pound bags of Rapid Set concrete mix, a bucket, a hoe for mixing, rubber gloves, a stiff-bristled brush, safety glasses, and dust masks. Honeyboy paid for everything in cash.

We hauled that stuff down to the basement and laid it out.

147

Neither of us had ever worked with concrete before, but I'd seen it mixed, and I knew the secret was not to add too much water. That would just make it thin and runny.

By the time we'd set everything up, it was getting dark.

While Honeyboy rigged some bedsheets to cover his great-great auntie's dearly departed roomies, I called Mom and told her I wouldn't be home for a couple of days, then I ordered two pizzas and a six-pack of Budweiser, and, while I awaited delivery, I surfed the internet on my cellphone, browsing YouTube clips on working with concrete. It didn't look like our project would be that tough, but my experience is nothing does until you actually start doing it.

We ate our pizzas off a plastic storage bin on the living room floor next to the pentagram carving. I was so hungry I wolfed down the slices in half-chewed globs, washing them down my gullet with foamy Bud. At that moment, it tasted better than an eight-course meal at the Lexington in St. Paul (not that I've ever actually eaten there, the place being too pricey for my wallet).

"So, what did you tell Vanessa?" I asked him, Vanessa being his wife.

"Told her the truth, that I'd be working day and night to get this place ready to list."

"And you told her the reason for this sudden urgency, what we found in the basement?"

His face darkened, cheese drippings on his orange beard. "I didn't tell her anything of the sort. Just told her we'd be hitting it hard to finish up. I'm sure she's glad to have me out of her hair for a few days."

We spent the rest of the evening in silence, clearing out the last of first floor and getting a start on the second. We threw out the beds but kept the mattresses to sleep on. It was after midnight when we finally crashed. I slept in a partially emptied upstairs bedroom. Honeyboy slept in the living room.

I'd brought a fifth of JD and a change of clothes in a canvas backpack. I considered popping the cork on the Jack, but was too tired. I knew that once I hit that mattress, I'd be dead to the world. Why waste a fine Kentucky sour-mash whiskey?

Besides, I had a sneaky feeling I'd be more in need of it the next night.

THE CEMENT FLOOR IN THE BASEMENT was four inches thick. I cut away a small square of it to get a look at the ground underneath. A rocky but fine soil lay below. I held a palmful out for Honeyboy to examine. "We shouldn't have any trouble digging through this," I said.

I maneuvered the saw, slow and steady, letting the blade do most of the work. It spewed a stream of cement grit into the air, making us glad we'd thought to buy dust masks and safety glasses. I was looking to carve out a hole about six feet by six feet, but I couldn't just cut out one big slab. It would be too hefty to haul up the stairs. Also, I knew I had to be careful not to rip blindly into any sewer or gas lines. It took me over two hours of carefully cutting the concrete into brick-sized portions (with a few breaks thrown in), and it gave me a real appreciation for anyone who had to do this kind of work for a living. My hands throbbed, arms ached, and I was covered in sweaty dust from head to toe.

Now that the area was bared of cement, it was digging time. "Grab us some shovels," I said to Honeyboy.

He found a pair of shovels under the stairs, one flat-nosed, one pointed, both rusty but sturdy and serviceable. We dug for another hour, the dug-out dirt rising in a mini dune on the far side of the hole, and got down about four feet before we called it quits for the day.

It was only maybe five at night, but you could only push your body to the breaking point. I was sore in muscles I didn't even know I had.

"We'll finish this up tomorrow," I said, not looking forward to moving the cadavers.

After washing up, we sat outside on the front step despite the brisk temps, drinking beers and not saying much. Finally, I suggested running over to Subway and picking up a couple a foot-longs while Honeyboy kept an eye on the place.

"Okay, but I'm not moving from this step until you get back."

There's a Subway sub shop at a strip mall in Golden Valley. I ordered a couple of veggie subs for me and a couple of roast beefs for

149

Honeyboy, along with some chips and fountain drinks. On the way back, I stopped at a liquor store and bought a twelve-pack of Old Milwaukee. Altogether, I couldn't have been gone more than forty-five minutes, but when I pulled up in front of Aunt Jolaine's house, it was already starting to get dark. Honeyboy was nowhere to be seen, and a black van was now parked in the driveway next to the dumpsters.

Feeling uneasy, but not yet ready to panic, I gathered the takeout carton and the twelve-pack, and bravely carried them to the front door. After all, the visitor could've been anyone. A realtor, a buddy. Maybe Vanessa dropped by to say hi. Maybe it wasn't ghostyard ghouls come to claim the seven moldering cadavers inside.

Setting down my armload on the floor, I crept through the blackened living room, listening keenly. Muffled conversation came from downstairs. As I neared the basement entrance, I saw light and shadows on the cement floor below. I wanted to call out to Honeyboy, but was too frightened. Instead, I cautiously descended.

"Take them! Take them, please. I'd be glad to be rid of them." Honeyboy's voice was pleading.

As I neared the foot of the stairs, I could see the shadows were being thrown from the backroom where the corpses hung, the tapestry of the howling man pulled to one side. I remembered Honeyboy had fetched the shovels from under the stairs, so I searched there for a tool of some kind to use as a weapon, if needed. I clasped the cold handle of a rake and carefully tugged it to my chest, but in the dark, metal shifted and squealed. Assorted gardening hardware crashed to the floor.

As I spun around, silhouetted forms swarmed at me. Holding the rake in a death grip, I swung it hard, connected with the first assailant, but when I hauled back for a second swing, hands clutched me. The rake clattered to the cement, and four figures yanked me from my feet and dragged me into the back chamber where Honeyboy, tied to an aluminum lawn chair, waited.

He had a frantic look in his eyes.

Two women and two men deposited me on the ground beside Honeyboy. A woman followed behind us, clasping the rake and a bleeding head wound.

They were all dressed for nightwork in black clothing and black, hooded robes. Some were middle-aged, two were well past their prime, and the one I'd clobbered with the rake looked barely in her twenties. They all shared a deadpan gaze that brought terror crawling up my back.

I started to get up when one of the older men, who'd now taken possession of the rake, pressed a foot firmly on my throat. Peering down threateningly, he reminded me of a painting of an angry god I'd once seen in a library book.

Using tin snips and hedge clippers, the others took on the wires that held the corpses against the wall. Once freed of their restraints, the dead were laid down with care.

"What do you want with those things, anyway?" I asked, the foot still on my neck.

Without a word in reply, they finished cutting the last of the cadavers loose and, wrapping them each in black canvas, carried them, one by one, up the stairs.

"What are you going to do to us?" I asked my captor, who remained behind.

His lips started stirring, like he was about to answer, when Honeyboy, in a sudden move, burst from the chair. Bent aluminum piping and polyester webbing skidded across the cement. Honeyboy's wrists jerked free of the cord that bound them, and before either the rake-holder or I could react, he was out of the room, scrambling through the gloomy basement.

"Stay here!" The angry god scowled down at me before removing his foot from my throat and hurrying after Honeyboy.

I was up in a flash, joining the chase.

Honeyboy's pursuer swung the rake and batted him to the floor. As I came up behind the two of them, I heard yelling from the kitchen and a clattering of footsteps on the basement stairs. Leveling a flying tackle into the rake-swinger's back, I brought him down hard. He rolled over, and I saw where the rake's tines had cut into his arm. He pawed the wound, groaning.

Hustling over to Honeyboy, I tried lifting him, but he was dead weight, out for the count.

Then the others, in a flurry of flapping fabric, grasping fingers, and fist blows, descended on me like an angry lynch mob.

I kicked and punched, elbowed and kneed, left to right and back again in the ominous basement, sometimes connecting, sometimes just hacking through air. I'm not sure what happened, but I became a dynamo, and I remember thinking, *no way are these crazy fuckers pinning me down again.*

Plowing through a gap in my assailants, I made for the stairs and clambered up them, emerging into the dark interior of the house. I could hear the ghouls following me, but once I was in the living room, I felt I might be home free.

The front door flew open, and I was bolting through the tufted lawn, rushing instinctively across the street to the house with the hamsa—the Bassetts—and hammering on their screen door. I didn't know what else to do. At first, I didn't think anyone was going to answer, which I guess I couldn't have blamed them for. I mean, some wacko stranger pounding on their door in the gathering night? Anyone would be hesitant to answer.

Finally, someone did, opening the inner door a few inches, the chain guard still in place. A worried-looking teenage girl stood eyeing me like I was the Boston Strangler.

From behind me came a scampering. My first thought was that they were after me. But I was wrong. The ghouls piled in the van, screamed out of Aunt Jolaine's driveway, and peeled off into the night. I turned back to the teen who was still staring at me, wide-eyed and open-mouthed.

"Sorry to have bothered you," I said, and headed back across the street.

HONEYBOY WAS ALRIGHT. He ended up dazed with some nicks and scrapes, but nothing serious. Once he was feeling like himself again, we cracked open the Old Milwaukees and nibbled a bit on the sandwiches, too jazzed to really be hungry.

"Do you think they'll come back?" he asked.

We'd taken our repast to the front step. Across the street at the Bassetts' house, curtains twitched.

"For what? They got what they came for."

"For … I don't know … us?"

We looked at each other with the weight of the world now on our shoulders.

I thought for a minute. The logical part of my brain was assuring me they had no reason to bother us anymore, but the emotional part remained unconvinced. "Let's say, from now on, we only work here during the daylight."

Honeyboy rubbed a rope burn on his wrist. "Alright."

"We fix the basement floor, empty all the rooms, and leave it at that."

"Yeah, and?"

"And we put the place on the market, as is."

The way Honeyboy looked at me, I couldn't tell if he was puzzled or still a touch dazed. "As is?"

"As is," I said. "And take whatever we can get for it."

He chewed on this for a while before answering in a defeated tone, "*Al-right.*"

The cloudless night sky held up a three-quarters moon bright enough to cast the neighborhood in a ghostly glow. Inside houses up and down the block, New Hope residents would be going about their evening routines, unaware—or in the Bassetts' case, unsure—of what had transpired on the suburban grounds so near their home sweet homes. We sat there, taking it all in, drinking our beers, quiet as the night breeze. Thoughts of strung-up corpses and hooded ghouls surfaced again and again in our minds' eyes. We must have sat in silence for almost an hour.

Finally, I could see it was up to me to break our lethargy.

"Let's get the hell out of here," I said. "That's enough excitement for one night."

153

# THE DAY OF THE DEAD

"Nathanael looked into Clara's eyes; but it was death whose
gaze rested so kindly upon him."
—E.T.A. Hoffmann, "The Sandman"

He was in Mexico City sipping a carajillo at the café El
Ojo de Madera when he learned about the old woman.
The peal of his cellphone cut through the mariachi
Muzak and the chatter from the dozens of middle-class
patrons gathered around tile-top tables.

"Hello?" Fast Benny Santiago, all hundred and twenty-five
pounds of him, in an ageless tan suit and pork pie hat, bent
forward to hear better. "Roger?"

The connection was terrible, so Benny tossed some coins on
the table and walked out of the café, moving surprisingly smooth
and poised for a Latino man pushing sixty.

"Okay, Roger, I can hear you now."

"Benny, I hate to be the one to break it to you, but the old girl's
gone."

"Imelda? Gone…"

"As in 'to meet her maker.'"

Outside, dusk was about to fall on an overcast day. There was
sufficient chill in the air for the strollers on the crowded redbrick
pedestrian corridor to be wearing light jackets or open coats. On
either side of the walkway, lining the building facades, huddled
skeletal tables packed with customers.

"How did it happen?" Benny asked.

On the other end of the line, Roger Molinar, one of Benny's dearest friends, cleared his throat. "The big C. Ovarian cancer, I think. Her funeral is Friday."

"You going?"

"Probably not. You?"

"No. I'm in Mexico. Tomorrow is el Día de los Muertos. Day of the Dead. I came to have a little vacation. Looks like half the gringos in America had the same idea. Anyway, I promised someone I'd run an errand for them while I'm here."

"Errand?"

"For my cousin. You remember Miguel."

"The drug dealer?"

"That was his son Mikey. Miguel is in the produce business. Anyway, I promised him I'd take care of something."

Roger paused. "If you were here, would you have gone to the funeral?"

"Probably not." The old woman's withered, putty-colored image suddenly appeared crisp and clear in Benny's mind, sucking the wind from him for a minute, her teeth stained brownish from coffee and cigarettes, her hair copper-colored and wiry, that diabolic glimmer in her eyes. "Anyway, I've got to go. Thanks for calling, Roger. Let's shoot some eight-ball at Two Stooges when I get back."

"Sure thing, Benny. Sorry about—" He paused again. "Sorry about everything. Take it easy, my man. Don't get mixed up in anything down there you can't get unstuck from."

"Don't worry. You know me. Always got my head on a swivel. See you."

*The old girl is gone.*

He knew what the words meant but was having trouble making sense of them. It was like someone saying a mountain or a city or a force of nature was gone. It required a wholesale reevaluation

155

of reality. Somehow it seemed a different world without her, though undoubtedly an improved one.

*Imelda Abalos has left the building.*

He'd expected to get a call like this one day, but he'd never expected its impact would be like getting hit by a Mack truck. True, the old woman was as close to being a mother to him as anyone had ever been. But that didn't excuse her.

Benny let the altered reality wash over him as he headed down the street, hands in his pockets. The sight of a dingy pool hall buoyed his spirits briefly. A young man, smiling wide, leaned over crimson felt, talking up a raven-haired senorita in a Metallica T-shirt and blue jeans. Maybe that's what he needed. Hand over the cards, then go shoot a little stick. Maybe have a beer or two. Hell, he was on vacation, wasn't he?

Walking in this crowd was like being carried by a stream. It required minimal effort, and his progress was dependent on shifts and swirls largely beyond his control. That's alright. At the moment, he was content to drift along.

Signs and banners proclaiming tomorrow's festivities draped lampposts, storefronts, and restaurants. Revelers jumping the gun were already wearing Day of the Dead costumes. A skull-faced merrymaker passed by, smoking a fat cigar through the breathing hole of his plastic mask. Grim brain-casings leered down on the crowd from decorative murals.

*How gleefully his people celebrated death. Maybe they had the right idea.*

As he walked on for several blocks, the crowd slowly reduced to a trickle—knots of humanity strolling the evening calm: hand-holding couples, jabbering matrons, aged loners, sweet-smelling young ladies with paper roses behind their ears, half-drunk gauchos, a shabby bum. A few dark-eyed boys wandered toward Benny, headed for the festivities down the road. As they passed, the streetlights lit, casting murky shadows in doorways and alleys.

This portion of the commercial district featured businesses that closed at night: a print shop, a travel agency, a post office. Here the buildings were taller and narrower, many embellished with religious carvings, Day of the Dead figurines, and spray-painted gang graffiti.

At last, he came to the dimly lit side street where Lázaro Delgado lived. This was a residential area of plus-size houses with grassy verges, fences, stunted trees, and decorative accent walls. SUVs, sedans, and minivans lined the streets and driveways.

Light spilled on lawns through plateglass windows. It was still early, so most of the houses showed some activity: people eating, talking, many gathered around television sets. Here and there, Day of the Dead parties were already in full gear, bone folks and ghouls drinking from goblets while muffled hip-hop and rock tunes hummed in the night. Children ran around one house, chasing each other and giggling. In the distance, several dogs barked.

There was no discernable activity at Lázaro's abode, a sprawling, two-story sand-colored structure where every window was shuttered with aluminum blinds. A sidewalk—whimsically reminiscent in shape of the Yellow Brick Road—wound to his steps.

Benny followed it to a front outer door with bars that resembled gothic colonnades and rang the doorbell.

Lázaro, a short man in a house robe, looked nothing like his picture on the government website. His cheeks were gaunter, his eyes duller, his hair grayer and ill-trimmed, his skin more rugged, leathery, and sun-starved.

"Miguel Santiago sent me with these." Benny held out the plastic debit cards: ten cards in five-hundred-dollar increments. "He said this would speed up getting the necessary clearances for his avocado trucks."

"I know who you are, Mr. Benny," came his reply. "Let's take this inside." He held wide the door, checked to see if anyone outside was watching, then ushered Benny in.

Benny had hoped for a quick turnover. Hand Lázaro the cards, maybe exchange leery nods, then vanish into the night, quick and clean, this bit of nastiness behind him. But Lázaro seemed to have other ideas.

"Sure." What else could Benny say?

In the entryway hung a large painting of a pink-and-dun-striped Gila monster coiled on a desert rock. The creature's black-lipped, triangular face all but jeered at him as Benny stepped past. The rug on the foyer's floor featured stylized chameleons in an Aztec motif, and the lamp that hung in the living room's threshold blazed with bug-eyed, art nouveau geckos.

But it was in the adjacent room that the true prize of Lázaro's obsession awaited: a humongous terrarium paneled in four-foot-tall glass sheets, two feet deep, resting on a wooden base that doubled its height. The enclosure, lit with rows of cold neon lights, was glutted with fauna, driftwood, and motley stones, as well as dozens of scaley, jewel-eyed inhabitants. Aside from the meager threshold lamp, only the terrarium lit the gloomy room, which also contained a sofa, end tables, and an armchair.

Turning to his host, Benny began, "I see lizards—"

But before he could finish the sentence, an illusion flickered: Lázaro's face turned pea-soup green and cornified into myriad patterned diamonds, and the eyes became lidless and oversized, with vertical pupils. The overall effect was serpentine. It quickly passed, though, and Lázaro reverted at once to his human features.

Benny blamed shadow play in the murky room; perhaps contributed to by lingering jet lag from yesterday's flight from Minnesota. Still, the sight left him dumbstruck; the vision of soulless snake eyes burned in his memory.

158

"Lizards? Yes. In fact, all things reptilian. It's my hallmark, you see?" He stepped to the terrarium and tapped on the glass. "These beings fascinate me. Always have. Something about their expressionless stare. You can never tell what one is thinking. Before you arrived, I was sitting in the dark, just watching them. I could watch for hours."

Benny swallowed. The old woman had also loved reptiles, though on a smaller scale. The first time he'd entered her home, looking for a warm place to sleep for the night, he'd been drawn at once (as any boy would be) by her many fishbowls of turtles and garter snakes.

"I used to have a four-line snake named Slithers," she'd told him that day. "Four feet long and beautifully colored. Tamest snake you've ever seen. All the children loved him, and he loved them. You could just tell. They carried him around in their arms and on their shoulders, petted him, fed him small rabbits and mice. I used to sleep with him. Then he went and died on me. I sometimes still miss my old Slithers."

A pensive smile had etched her wrinkled face.

"Listen, I should really be going," Benny said now to Lázaro.

"Nonsense," came his reply. "Sit down. We'll have a drink to toast our newfound friendship."

"I'm not much of a drinker."

Lázaro's eyes blazed and, for the briefest instant, again appeared to gleam reptilian. "Tonight," said the bureaucrat, "you drink."

Benny sank to the couch as his host walked to the kitchen.

Left alone with his thoughts in the dreary living room, Benny weighed the pros and cons of darting for the door. On the plus side, he'd be free of this shady official, this creepy house, and, hopefully, the reoccurring delusions that plagued him here. On the negative side, he'd look like a fool and possibly cast uncertainty over Miguel's avocado deal with this guy. Five thousand bucks and the admittedly trifling vestiges of Benny's machismo were at stake.

*One drink, and that's it. One drink, and I'm out of here.*

"You are in for a real treat, my friend," Lázaro said, carrying in two tumblers of gold-colored liquor and two slices of an orange. "This mezcal is from the finest distillery in Oaxaca. It's made from specially cultivated agave, from a breed said to be hundreds of years old. And the Mezcalero is a descendant of the great Mexican General Pancho Villa."

Benny fought to steady his hands as he took the glass and orange slice from Lázaro.

"This is something very rare. Something you can tell your American friends about. I think you'll find it quite flavorful."

"Thanks," Benny said, awkwardly gripping the slippery tumbler.

Mezcal, cousin of tequila. Tequila had also been a favorite of Imelda Abalos.

It was past midnight when he'd knocked the secret knock that allowed him to enter her nest. As soon as she answered, he saw she was three sheets to the wind.

By the time he was maybe eleven years old, he'd been staying with the old girl off and on for about a year. He lived there with a series of other boys who also rotated indiscriminately in and out of Imelda's domicile, as was the custom. Even back then, they'd referred to her as the old girl. She couldn't have been much older than forty at the time, though she looked eons older, boozing and villainy no doubt having taken their toll on her appearance.

"Benny," she'd said. "My Benny boy. What have you brought me tonight?"

He'd held out the tributes for her to see: the timepiece swiped from the downtown Dayton's, the bag of ripple chips she so enjoyed, the few crumpled bills he'd managed to pull together

160

from selling at the pawn shop the harmonica he'd won for reading the most books in his sixth-grade class.

Bracing herself on the edge of the door, she crinkled her nose at these offerings but let him in nonetheless.

"Roger's here," she said. "Hawk and Dmitri, too. Luca's out earning at the moment, but I expect him back shortly."

Luca was the only boy who permanently lived at Imelda's. Luca was the old girl's favorite.

Benny knew the others would be sleeping. It was a school night. He wanted nothing more than to crawl onto an empty mattress himself, but he couldn't leave until she dismissed him.

"Keep me company for a minute, Benny boy," she said. "Just until Luca comes home. He'll be back any minute."

He laid the tributes on the dining-room table and slid out a chair. Benny was dog-tired and had school in the morning, but having a safe place to lay his head that night was more important. He'd listen to the old girl ramble on, not saying much himself, just making little throat noises of agreement now and then.

She poured herself a tall shot glass of Jose Cuervo and was about to rifle it when she stopped and looked at him as if just noticing his presence.

"Have you ever tasted tequila, Benny?" Her eyes, glazed and vaguely malevolent, examined him curiously.

"Uh-uh." *How many children had?*

"Well, then, let me educate you."

A second shot glass was laid on its side, having leaked remnants of liquid onto the tabletop. She righted it, filled it out, and pushed it toward Benny.

"Bottoms up," she'd said.

And, trustingly, he'd lifted the rim to his lips.

NOW LÁZARO, SMILING BROADLY, settled in the living room's armchair, careful not to spill from his glass. "Legend tells us mezcal is the holiest of liquors. That it comes from an ancient Zapotec goddess."

Benny sniffed the tumbler. A faint smoky scent wafted up at him.

"They say that worms entered the goddess' body one day and nestled in her heart. Their presence changed the milk in her forty-thousand breasts into a powerful liquor. All who partook of her breast milk after said it was delicious and potent. The goddess, being of a kind and generous nature, decided to share this new intoxicant with all of humankind. Using her magic powers, she transferred the liquid's essence into a lightning bolt she hurled from the sky, striking an agave plant, splitting it open, and releasing the plant's altered juices. And that's how this wonderful beverage came to us. Straight from the wormy heart of a goddess. I can't testify to the truth of this legend, but the story is the reason mezcal is known as the 'elixir of the gods.'"

Lázaro clinked glasses with Benny. They cocked back their heads, brought the tumblers to their lips, then gunned the fiery liquor down their gullets. To Benny, it felt like gulping liquid smoke mixed with flaming embers. He sucked madly on the orange slice, the pulpy sweetness doing little to relieve the burning blossoming in the pit of his stomach.

Benny fanned his tongue with his porkpie hat. "Whoo-hoo." Through watering eyes, he watched Lázaro's grinning teeth sharpen and grow to the length of a forefinger. The mirage was perfect, down to the venom dripping from Lázaro's glistening fangs.

Then Benny's vision cleared, and the bureaucrat's smile resumed human dimensions.

"I-I really must be leaving." Padding his protest with a lie, he added, "I'm supposed to meet some friends at El Ojo de Madera." He checked the time display on his cellphone. "I'm already running late."

"One more drink," Lázaro replied, "then I promise to cut you free, Mr. Benny, to meet up with your friends. Relax. The night is still young."

He rose, collected his guest's tumbler and orange rind, and slipped off again into the kitchen before Benny could further object.

A new strangeness settled on the slender, aged Latino. In the glow of the terrarium, the edges and corners of the room and all that was in it turned softer and rounder. Sparks of light like fireflies glimmered and extinguished in the dark. The sofa he sat in appeared to be melting beneath him, but he felt no need to extricate himself. The elixir of the gods coursed in his veins, spreading warmth and tranquility to his extremities, turning his bones rubbery, making the flesh on his face begin to sag. The lizards behind the glass fixed their jeweled eyes upon him, eager to witness the next act of this play in which he now starred.

In this interval, Lázaro was gone for what seemed an eternity, though Benny no longer trusted his sense of time. The urgency he'd felt earlier had suddenly dissipated. Now, he was happy to wait in the soothing darkness on the melting sofa with the mystic fireflies. He let his mind wander.

That night at the old girl's house, when he'd tasted his first sips of tequila, her creased hand had crawled across the table toward him like a mottled salamander approaching a cricket, coming to rest at last on the smooth, puerile flesh of his arm, gently prodding and caressing it. "My lovely boy," she'd said. "You could give so much pleasure."

As she slinked her chair closer to his, her hand crept to his belly, which was both clenched in fear and tingly with presentiment. He watched, frozen, as she lifted his shirt and lightly stroked his skin to the crest of his zippered blue jeans. The next thing he knew, she'd brought him to the floor, flat on his back, his breath hitching with apprehension. Smelling of cigarette

163

smoke, she'd bent to kiss him, her ancient tongue, the color of organ flesh, groping toward his lips, between his teeth and into his mouth, squirming swollen and sticky.

Now Lázaro, returning with the refilled tumblers, stood over Benny, grinning again with his snake teeth.

Benny waved him back. "I think I've had enough," he said in the voice of a terrified eleven-year-old.

The bureaucrat's face resumed its snakelike pigment and texture. "Drink," he commanded, holding out the glass. "I insist."

Benny took the glass as Lázaro's eyes assumed their serpent countenance. This was no flicking illusion, no trick of the light. This appeared to be a genuine transformation, a metamorphosis of Faustian proportions. In the dim living room, hovering over Benny, towered the reptilian-veneered devil himself, tempting with the apple of knowledge; the deadly rattlesnake Hopi warriors danced with and carried in their mouths to the hypnotic beat of drums; the Aztec god Quetzalcoatl, poised to tear apart the giant sea monster whose remnants would form the earth and the sky.

Tears already running down his cheeks, Benny lifted the tumbler to his lips with a shaking hand. The concoction—mezcal or whatever it might be—splashed down his throat in a fiery swirl, his stomach threatening but unable to eject it. Not only did it radiate throughout his bloodstream, but it shined ghostlike from beneath his skin and clothing. He threw back his head and arms, surrendering to the jolt of the potent liquid. It plowed through him with the force of an ocean wave. He collapsed inside himself, protruded outside himself, and somehow stumbled to his feet, awash in a chaotic blend of euphoria and sweat-popping fear.

One wall of the living room became images that repeated themselves to infinity. The ceiling opened on a night sky of flame-streaking comets. The terrarium tottered precipitously, the neon lights fluttering, the captive lizards pulsing like flattened jellyfish against the glass.

For Lázaro, the snake transformation was now complete. He writhed on the floor, fat as a rundlet barrel and nearly as long as the room's full length. His lidless, vertical pupils studied Benny. A forked tongue emerged from the snake man's mouth, wriggling as if to taste Benny's presence.

Grabbing his cellphone and porkpie hat, Benny dragged his feet toward the entryway.

The terrarium crashed to the floor, landing on the huge snake, instantly dividing it like mercury into hundreds of baby snakes that squirmed like maggots as the freed lizards scampered over them. The neon lights flicked off, and now the room was lit only by the glow of the fireflies and the tails of the streaking comets overhead.

Benny lost his footing and tumbled through the door onto the grassy lawn outside. To his left, the Yellow Brick Road sidewalk wriggled out to the street.

All the houses up and down the road began emptying of people, and the former inhabitants dropped to the ground and crawled on their bellies like lizards, like salamanders. They streamed into the dim street and wound past parked cars, stunted trees, and Benny, as if in the grip of some hypnotic thrall: children, some in their pajamas, others in play clothes, some even in diapers; men in assorted dress, blue jeans and work shirts mostly, but some in housecoats, some in underwear, one man naked; women in culottes, skirts, denim pants; revelers in Day of the Dead costumes. Young and old, squirming on their bellies, filing down the street, looking straight ahead as if drawn to a fixed location in the direction opposite the city street where Benny had drunk his carajillo in the café.

He watched with fascination, a starstruck spectator of this macabre parade.

Where were they going? Did it matter? Ultimately, aren't we all slithering to the same finish line?

He shook his head, but it refused to clear.

From behind the rows of houses sprang searchlights that swept the sky, catching on occasional shards of cloud and on swells of smoke rolling in from distant factories where, even on the eve of the Day of the Dead, workers toiled to feed the ever-famished maw of industry. A weather siren rent the night with ominous warning. A cool breeze rushed the air.

Benny pulled on his hat, watching as the crowd of spellbound Mexicans groveled past. Then he, too, began to crawl. Toward them. What else could he do?

A gap opened in the throng for him, and he entered, feeling a part of something he could not understand: faceless, mindless, on his stomach on the gritty tar of the street, relieved of responsibility by the anonymity of the crowd for all acts committed to and by him, Fast Benny Santiago, past, present, and future.

Just another member of the reptilian night surge.

WHEN HE OPENED HIS EYES, it was the following day, and sunlight assailed him. He touched his head to ensure his hat was still there, which it was, then sat up from his slouched position on a wooden bench along the side of a jam-packed street. The palms of his hands throbbed and were bloody, as were his knees, which were exposed by the ruptured cloth of his pants. His tan jacket and the front of his shirt were filthy and torn, and the skin beneath stung.

In front of him, a mariachi band of revenants in huge sombreros and black waistcoats marched past, playing their instruments. On the bench beside him, a beautiful Mexican boy done up like Caspar the Friendly Ghost gaped at him, fingering snot from a nostril. The boy's mother, wearing funeral garb, eyed Benny with disgust and pulled the child closer to her in a protective gesture.

His first coherent thought was of the bum he'd passed while walking to Lázaro's house. *Yes, that's how I must look to them. A derelict imposing on their festive day with my grubby clothes and hungover manner.*

He checked to make sure he hadn't lost his wallet or hotel key. He hadn't. Well, that was something. Feeling unwelcome on the bench, he rose and began roaming through the masses of parade-goers that crowded the borders of the street.

Most of the assembled wore at least some token of acknowledgment to the grim day: morbid T-shirts, grisly pins, skeletal pendants, black roses, mascara thick in the hollows of their eyes, and so on. Others presented themselves full-bore Grateful Dead, their faces painted or masked in eggshell white, tattooed with scars and kaleidoscopic sigils, their skulls fruiting colorful flowers. Some cloaked themselves in somber shrouds, some in cerements more psychedelically flavored. There were widows' peaks of spiderwebs, sleeves of flesh-stripped bone, eyes with piercing whites blazing from behind dark veils, feathered bowlers, ebony walking sticks crowned with crystal brain pans.

A monstrous Madonna in a graveyard bonnet waved to Benny from atop a pageant float as she passed by. *Wait a minute, was that...* No. Just a lingering hallucination from whatever Lázaro had doped him with last night. *She was gone. Remember? The old girl was gone.* Men bearing executioner's hoods and glistening axes marched behind the float, and behind them clopped ancient, sad-sack horses carrying ghostly Don Quixotes.

He bought a Chiapas coffee from a street vendor and, as he walked and sipped, began cobbling together fragments of memory from the preceding night. He struggled to clear his head from what felt like the remnants of rot-gut whiskey combined with the waning effects of mescaline.

Once again, the crowd carried him along.

He recalled crawling on his belly with the others last night, not knowing why, not caring. He'd relinquished all logic and understanding to embrace that new reality, that new way of being, and in that moment, he'd felt freer than ever before.

As they'd crawled to the outskirts of town, the houses narrowed and lengthened and spiraled into steepled towers with outer staircases that wound like piano keys to darkened belfries where barely visible men and women in turbans and fezzes and fringed, palm-leafed hats silently watched their progress. Gradually, the street had reduced to a crushed-rock trail that tracked past neighborhoods of burnt ruins, vacant except for the scaley newts and toads peering at them from the ledges of glassless windows.

They'd made their way into a weed-choked lot dotted with monoliths tall as mountains, in the midst of which squatted a lichen-encrusted water well made of stone blocks.

One by one, they'd clambered to the well and over the stone edge and dropped into the abyss within. When his turn came, he'd slipped into the well's mouth without a moment's hesitation. Rather than plunging as a human being might be expected to do, he sank almost languidly into the velvety darkness, like a tiny creature drifting in the wind.

Looking up, he'd expected to see fellow crawlers tumbling after him, but instead he saw a face smiling down on him. Imelda Abalos. Not the lecherous, tequila-sodden old girl who'd crudely defiled him that night on the living room floor, but Imelda in a previous incarnation: the Imelda who'd taken him in when he had no other place to go, who'd filled his empty stomach with food, and made him safe and warm. What a comfort that withered face had brought him then. Imelda before the sinister glint had fully entered her eyes, and her coppery hair had become a wiry, viperous tangle, and her brown-stained teeth had turned into fangs.

Though she'd led him far astray, some part of him still loved her.

Her face then gradually dwindled to a speck, and then to nothingness. The soothing pitch had nestled him as he continued his journey down, down, down.

And that was all he remembered of the previous night, except for a vision that came to him in that long, dark passage that seemingly meandered to the center of the earth. It was of the last time he'd seen her: that morning on the sidewalk in front of her house when the New Hope police had frog-marched her in handcuffs to their waiting squad car. Her, weary and disheveled in a soiled robe, looking lost and frightened, not recognizing him, not recognizing Roger or any of the other boys either, not even Luca, her favorite.

This sight of her, broken and confused, made it impossible for Benny to muster the hatred for her that he felt entitled to.

Now, in the sun on a crowded street in Mexico City on the Day of the Dead, Fast Benny, drinking his coffee and lost in thought, ambled along those hazy lines that divide the past from the present, reality from illusion, the world of the living from the world of the dead—all of which had become, in this moment, indistinguishable from one another.

# Acknowledgments

I first read Edgar Allan Poe in grade school. Even at that early age I was dumbstruck by the power of the man's writing. I hear he's falling out of favor with many academics these days (along with Robert Louis Stevenson and other brilliant writers), but, for my money, Poe is still the master. He brings clarity and insight to the haunted mind like no one since. I still get a thrill from reading his stories.

The reason I'm writing about dear Edgar is I'm often asked what writers influenced me and I figured this was as good a place as any to set the record straight.

My other literary mentors tend to be old school with a slightly weird bent: Nathaniel Hawthorne, Franz Kafka, William Hope Hodgson, Guy de Maupassant, Stevenson, Ambrose Bierce, Algernon Blackwood, William Faulkner, and H.P. Lovecraft, to name a few. Among more modern writers, I especially enjoy Joyce Carol Oates, Thomas Ligotti, Ramsey Campbell, Stephen King and Cormac McCarthy (*Blood Meridian* is my favorite novel), to name but a few.

Little known fact: that year in grade school when I got turned on to Poe, I won an award for reading the most books in the class that year, which I never expected. My prize was a harmonica (just like Fast Benny Santiago in "The Day of the Dead") and I played it all the way home.

*Pale Blades of Moonlight* is the seventh book I've written. Most of them have been edited by Danita Mayer, whom I heartily recommend to writers everywhere. Her polishing puts the shine on my writing, and I cannot thank her enough.

I'd also like to thank my proofreader Jennifer Thompson, for catching my flubs and always having my back; my wife Debbie for sticking with me and supporting me in all my oddball ways; Paul Cochran for being a faithful reader; and all of those who have written nice reviews of my books. As we Buddhists like to say: I wish you all good health, success and happiness.

If you enjoyed *Pale Blades of Moonlight*, consider recommending it to your neighbors and friends on social media. Also, reader reviews are the lifeblood of modern publishing, and posting a brief review on Amazon, Goodreads or your favorite readers' blog would help a struggling author immeasurably.

For updates on my work, and other readings on dark fiction, check out my website at: www.joepawlowskiauthor.com. You can follow me on Facebook @ Joe Pawlowski, Author or on Instagram @ joepawlowskiauthor.

# Let the Terror Continue

OTHER BOOKS BY JOE PAWLOWSKI

### *Echoes From a Shoreless Void*
A curious souvenir unleashes a yearning that reaches from beyond the grave. Father Christmas transforms into an ancient ogre with malicious intent. A search for enlightenment leads down a horrifying trail of retribution.

Among these eleven stories there are scales, fangs, and claws; flashing blades and bellowing gun barrels; ghosts and demons of assorted forms and dispositions; and physical embodiments of envy, guile and overpowering lust.

Available from Amazon in paperback and ebook. Free on Kindle Unlimited.

### *In the Heart of the Garden Is a Tomb*
Nine nerve-tingling tales of the weird, the supernatural and the bizarre. Three friends lost on backwoods logging trails stumble on an ancient graveyard where a monster sentry from long ago await. A woman who struggles with a terrible loss finds she can only save her sanity by taking drastic action. A retiree, empowered by a gun found in his garbage can, learns that becoming a man of action isn't all it's cracked up to be.

These and other lost souls are only seeking a way out of their dire circumstances. But there's no escaping the bitter truth that awaits us all in the heart of the garden.

Available from Amazon in paperback and ebook. Free on Kindle Unlimited.

### *Why All the Skulls Are Grinning*
A shaken teenage girl, lost and abandoned at the gateway to another realm. A man driven mad by isolation who believes he's built an automaton to lead him back to open skies. A car salesman whose

girlfriend winds up a sacrificial offering to a rock god's dark deity. The stories contained in Why All the Skulls Are Grinning look into these tortured lives and many others.

Why are all the skulls grinning? Could it be because they have to smile to keep from shrieking?

Available from Amazon in paperback and ebook. Free on Kindle Unlimited.

### The Cannibal Gardener

A gardener with a secret life, a Goth woman with a morbid fascination, a serial killer who leaves a trail of bodies across the Midwest: they all come together at a Minnesota lakehouse in a transformation as evil as it is shocking.

*The Cannibal Gardener* combines out-of-this-world horror with a love story and a touch of grim humor from a master storyteller.

Available from Amazon in paperback and ebook, and on audiobook from Amazon, Audible and iTunes. Free on Kindle Unlimited.

### The Vermilion Book of the Macabre

From author of *The Cannibal Gardener* and *Dark House of Dreams* comes this highly anticipated collection of 16 spellbinding tales of supernatural suspense.

Readers call it "a blood-chilling collection" and say of Pawlowski "he paints his dark tales so realistically you will have nightmares."

Available from Amazon in paperback and ebook. Free on Kindle Unlimited.

### The Watchful Dead

A 12-year-old boy housebound all his life, a conjure woman who speaks to the dead, an evil slave trader driven ruthless by greed and a war hero whose greatest battles take place in his own mind: all are about to have their lives shaken to the core by powerful forces from beyond the grave.

Readers are calling it "a ride right off the bat" and "nicely written, with a lyrical quality that kept me turning virtual pages," and the author "possesses the talents of a classic great writer."

The Horror Review says *The Watchful Dead* is "a gutsy, ambitious, skillful exploration of cosmic/epic dark fantasy."

Available from Amazon in paperback and ebook. Free on Kindle Unlimited.

### *Dark House of Dreams*

In a city overrun by ghosts, fear lurks around every corner.

Add a murder plot, a devastating earthquake, a missing mother, a gang of outrageous villains, and a young boy tormented by demons both real and imagined, and you have an epic quest through the hidden places of monsters and gods.

Readers say it's a "well-written and creepy" journey that begins with a secret revealed in a charnel cave and ends with a hard-earned lesson learned in a *Dark House of Dreams*.

Available from Amazon in paperback and ebook. Free on Kindle Unlimited.

Can't get enough of *Pale Blades of Moonlight*?


Award-winning author Joe Pawlowski never fails to deliver

supernatural suspense and otherworldly thrills.


Enjoy this excerpt from

*In the Heart of the Garden Is a Tomb*

# The Pact

"Happiness is in the happy. But honor is not in the honored."
—Thomas Aquinas

Six mirrors lined the little round room, facing the center where Alessandro Yezdan stood at the altar, slicing the palm of his hand with a keen-edged black dagger. As blood welled up in the open cut, he made a fist and squeezed droplets of the vital fluid into a smoking, brass-plated censer. The blood sizzled on the glowing embers of incense.

"From the wide, ancient skies of Baala Sheem, where storm gods unsheathe swords of lightning, I call upon Valafar, succubus supreme in the nightmare army of Thamuz, queen of falsehoods."

He picked up the handbell from the altar's surface and shook it three times. Its peals echoed jarringly in the tiny chamber.

"Valafar, who causes all shadows to fall, come from your coven of three, from the deep roots of your shoreless void to the side of your True Believer. I beg you, come to me."

Alessandro, with his heavy eyebrows and hooked Italian nose, lifted bulging eyes skyward and dropped to his knees. His pockmarked face was the color of faded leather, and his grimace revealed stumps and crags of rancid brown teeth.

In the open portal overhead—hazy with the remnant smoke of late-summer fires blazing many miles to the north—appeared a great fluttering hawk who landed on the rim of the opening and peered down at him malevolently. From her sharp, curved beak, the bird dropped a tender twig of green leaf onto the altar, just as the book said she would.

Alessandro stood, picked up the sprig, and added it to the contents of the smoldering censer.

Outside, thunder bellowed. A hard rain began to fall, drumming on the rooftop of his suburban home on Boone Avenue North in New Hope, Minnesota. Inside, the censer erupted in a flash of flame that quickly permeated the room with the charged scents of petrichor and ozone.

He looked up, his sight swimming with flickering black spots.

A bolt of lightning silhouetted the hawk, limning her predatory beak and talons. She leaned her feathered crown in as if deciding whether or not to strike at him.

Now came the tricky part: the sloughing off of his earthly form so that he might communicate in the astral realm with the summoned entity. This was where things could go terribly wrong if fate so willed it.

True, he had slipped from his skin bag before in nighttime forays to ethereal dream worlds, but this time it was different. This time, he knew from Crowley's book that Valafar would hold the reins on his very survival. She could either extend a span for him to cross over to her, or she could cast him into the black abyss where he would plummet forever.

Or, the book had pointedly warned, she could simply eat him.

Rolling the dice on his destiny, he lifted himself from the world of solidity and substance, shedding his homely skin with practiced ease.

But when he emerged, it wasn't anything like the dream realm he'd entered before. Here he was not weightless. Here he was not free to roam unguarded through courtyards and houses and straying city streets, expansive as the horizon, careless as a gypsy moth. Instead, here he felt the significant burden of the cosmos on his insignificant mortal shoulders.

He tremored before stars that blinked down at him like a million eyes, before twirling planets of murky haze that pivoted toward him on their axes, before howling cosmic winds and stinging sands and bursts of panicky shadow that flapped past him on all sides. And from the center of this tumult, on a silver trail of moondust, approached a figure grim and serene. She took the form of Diana, consort of Lucifer, huntress of celestial woodlands and plains, and her beauty was almost blinding.

"Who calls to Valafar from the world of men?" Her voice, dark and full, reverberated in his ears over the cacophony.

"I ... I." He struggled to lift his voice over the din. "Alessandro. Alessandro Yezdan."

She stood not a dozen yards from him, her slender feet poised at the silvery path's end, just beyond where the awful black chasm began its yawn toward Alessandro. He stared at her, at her arched eyebrows and the clean line of her nose, at her pert lips and her elegant neck and shoulders, at the citrine hair elaborately pleated and braided.

"No one has called to me from your world for some time, Alessandro." She tilted her head slightly. "Have you come to barter?"

Overwhelmed, he stammered out meaningless sounds before successfully seizing control of his voice. "Yes ... yes, exactly." The book had said to set his fears aside and make his case as clearly and concisely as possible, but now that seemed far easier said than done, especially amid this celestial roar.

*Here is my chance,* he thought. *Don't blow it.*

Grappling through his terror, he launched hesitantly into his story, gathering strength as he went: "That is, my father was a military man— a sergeant in the Army. I always wanted to be like him, but I hadn't the strength of character, and he saw through all my flaws, and I'm afraid I was a disappointment to him.

"I tried joining the military, but I washed out in basic training and returned home a failure. That failing haunted me for all my life. I went to college for a while, but that didn't stick either. I ended up drifting from one dead-end job to the next through the course of my entire life. I never married. I never made a mark on any kind upon my world."

He eyed the endless blackness that lay just beyond his feet and realized that if therein lay his fate, it would perhaps be appropriate.

"Go on," she prodded.

"On his death bed, I'll never forget the look on Father's face. It told me that, in his eyes, my life amounted to nothing. Absolutely nothing. And he was right. After his funeral, I decided to try one more time to make something of myself. It was too late to impress him, but I could still make my mark if I could only find a way."

Alessandro had long toyed with the esoteric. With tarot cards and Ouija boards, and mass-produced paperback books on magic. He'd put these in the same category as slasher films and lurid novels: merely entertainment, not to be taken too seriously. But what if there *was* something legitimate to the occult? What if beyond the

181

physical world there lay a dominion he could tap into for his self-betterment? If indeed true, he reasoned, then pursuing this path would be his most direct and potentially fruitful course of action.

"I saw no other option," he said. "I'd already passed the age of fifty and could feel the press of mortality. So, I decided to devote every free moment to the study of forbidden knowledge. I investigated book after book, the older, the better, and learned many things, but not the path to the total reformation for which I yearned. Then one day at a book fair, I came upon a slim volume called *The Secret Teachings of the Hermetic Order of the Golden Dawn*, alleged to have been written by Aleister Crowley, the self-proclaimed wickedest man in the world. Though familiar with his other books, which I'd found largely incomprehensible, this was one I'd never heard of before, and at first, I doubted its authenticity. The seller, who had no idea who the Golden Dawn or Crowley were, said he'd bought it as part of a lot at an estate sale in Bemidji. I took it off his hands for five dollars, thinking there might be something of value in it even it turned out to be a swindle. The seller, frankly, looked relieved to be rid of it.

"When I brought it home and had a chance to study its yellowing pages, I saw that it was part of a very limited edition, one of a hundred, which would make it the rarest book in my collection. It could be the only remaining copy in existence. As I thumbed through the profusely illustrated pages, it struck me that this was exactly what I'd been searching for."

He'd constructed his circular altar room in the attic of his house following the precise instructions in the book. He'd practiced the rituals laid out to establish and strengthen his esoteric powers. Over time, he learned to influence the weak-willed. He learned to bend fortune his way in minor circumstances. He even learned to make himself invisible to others for brief periods. When he felt sufficiently secure in these skills, he turned his attention to summoning.

"It took me more than a year of studying the step-by-step instructions of Crowley's book to give me sufficient power and courage—pitiful as they may be—to stand before you now, Valafar."

With a wave of her hand, she silenced the maelstrom around them and formed a rickety bridge that spanned the abyss and provided him with a way to her. "Approach," she said, gesturing with her chin and stepping back.

Without hesitation, Alessandro moved forward. He knew from the book he had to trust the bridge to hold, no matter how flimsy it seemed, no matter how great his fear of falling. He had to walk with headstrong purpose, or all his work would have been for naught. So, boldly, he marched across the span even as it swayed and groaned beneath him. Even as he passed through the moist and fetid breath of gaping eternity below.

As his feet came to rest on the far lip of spongy soil, he stood before her, not sure what to do next.

"I don't grant favors, Alessandro. I only make pacts. You understand that, don't you?"

"Yes."

"I can do things for you, but only if you do things for me."

"I understand."

"And you must be aware that what I demand of you may seem beyond what you are capable of providing. But if you fail to remit my chosen tariffs, the consequences for you will be tragic in the extreme."

"I understand."

She appraised him skeptically, then said, "You want to be a military man?"

"I want to be an *important* military man—a general. I want to be famous and admired for my wisdom and daring. I want to be wealthy and enjoy the rewards of being a wealthy man. I want powerful allies, a beautiful wife, and a lovely family. I want to be handsome and to live a long life. If you can grant me all this, I'll repay you anything you wish."

"Very well," she said. "But I warn you: do not fail to deliver on that promise."

That said, she waved her hands, and Alessandro Yezdan stepped into his all-new life.

Made in the USA
Monee, IL
25 June 2025

19793634R00111